YACHT HI-JACK

Newlyweds Linda and Martin Firth set out to track down Linda's beautiful but wayward older sister who has disappeared under mysterious circumstances while crewing as an extra hand on the yacht *Milady*'s return voyage from Baltimore in the United States to Plymouth, England. They soon find themselves embroiled in the dangerous and murky world of drug-running.

Books by Ralph Stephenson
in the Linford Mystery Library:

FESTIVAL DEATH
DOWN AMONG THE DEAD MEN

RALPH STEPHENSON

YACHT HI-JACK

Complete and Unabridged

LINFORD
Leicester

First published in Great Britain in 1996

First Linford Edition
published 1999

British Library CIP Data

Stephenson, Ralph
    Yacht hi-jack.—Large print ed.—
    Linford mystery library
    1. Sailing—Atlantic Ocean—Fiction
    2. Drug traffic—Fiction 3. Suspense fiction
    4. Large type books
    I. Title
    823.9′14 [F]

    ISBN 0–7089–5609–2

Published by
F. A. Thorpe (Publishing) Ltd.
Anstey, Leicestershire

Set by Words & Graphics Ltd.
Anstey, Leicestershire
Printed and bound in Great Britain by
T. J. International Ltd., Padstow, Cornwall

This book is printed on acid-free paper

1

Incident at Sea

The storm was over. The yacht, which was dipping easily through the light swell, carried her largest genoa and full main, the sails just filling in the beam wind. It was early afternoon and the sun blazed down. A few white clouds were spread across the sky towards the horizon and the steadily rising glass pointed to 'fair'.

The crew of three were relaxed and somnolent after a lunch of cold chicken and salad washed down with a glass of wine, part of the fresh provisions bought at their last port of call which they had left the previous day. The only one up and about was the youngest, a girl in her late twenties, wearing a bikini, sitting in the cockpit with a magazine, and keeping half an eye on the sails and the steering. Only half an eye was needed as the self-steering gear was keeping the boat comfortably on course and no early sail changes were likely to be called for.

The owner of the yacht, a man in his fifties, short and strongly built, was dozing in a quarter-berth below and just to port of the companionway that led down from the cockpit, his feet tucked away where the end of the bunk extended under the cockpit. It was a snug berth in rough weather and, given a minute to collect himself, he could turn out quickly to go on watch or take over when called in emergency. Dressed in a shirt and shorts, he was lying on top of the bedclothes, half asleep. The book he had been reading had slipped into the bunk beside him and his lower denture (which he took out for comfort whenever he turned in) was tucked out of sight beside the foam mattress. His glasses he had put on the narrow shelf above his head.

This bunk was in the main cabin and on the chart-table opposite, beside the saloon table, was Admiralty Chart No. 3272, Newfoundland/Bermuda, going halfway across the Atlantic. On it their noon position, marked by a tiny dot, showed the yacht some ninety miles northeast-by-east of Bermuda, their last port of call, on course for the Azores. As they sailed farther east they would transfer to Admiralty Chart No. 1, Plymouth/Canaries which included the Azores, a chart that would eventually take the yacht by a series of noon-position stepping-stones back to one of the big mooring-buoys for visitors below the Royal Western Yacht Club on a rocky shore near Plymouth Hoe.

The owner's wife, the third member of the crew, was asleep in the after-cabin. About the same age as her husband, her suntanned face and freckles went attractively even now with her naturally fair hair, though it failed to give her the gamin, tomboy air she had had in her teens and early twenties, especially now she had the heavy shoulders and hips of a goodliving, childless, middle-aged woman disposed to *embonpoint*. She was lying on the starboard bunk inside a summer sleeping-bag made of sheeting, and lying with her head to the cabin door, since the two bunks came together in a V-shape at the stern of the boat.

The girl in the cockpit looked into the cabins and, seeing the other two were asleep or somnolent, reached into a bag and took out a container holding white powder which she sniffed up eagerly. Her drug habit, recently acquired and as yet relatively uncomplicated, she kept from the other two. Then, desire satisfied, with a glance at the compass showing the ship's heading and a look round at the sails, she climbed out of the cockpit and lay down on the narrow deck, her magazine held in one hand, her bikini-top in the other, naked except for an inch of bathing-suit round her loins.

Earlier during lunch a large tanker had passed the yacht going south-east, probably on a direct route from New York to round the Cape of Good Hope, but now there was nothing on the horizon, not even a smudge of smoke. The only movement came from a school of porpoises that flickered like shadows round the bow, and from the yacht itself as it dipped gently forward, steered and moved by the gods of wind and water.

★ ★ ★

To disturb this peaceful scene there came the far-off noise of an engine. Not the deep double-bass thud of a cargo-boat's monster diesel, but the higher, insect-like hum of a fast motorboat. It was a fishing launch, its high-powered motors pushing it along at 15 knots, a plume of white surging at its bow. By the time the girl sat up and looked astern with a steady speculative gaze, it was well over the horizon, perhaps a mile-and-a-half from the yacht, six minutes away. It had come from the direction of their last port and it came up astern, making direct for the yacht, which moved along unruffled at about a third the speed.

The girl put on her bathing-top and went back to the cockpit where she watched it silently, awaiting its arrival with a kind of composure. When the engine noise was at its height and the launch was only a few minutes away, the man in the cabin called out, his eyes closed, still half asleep.

'What's that?'

'It's another boat,' said the girl in a soothing tone. 'Don't disturb yourself.'

'Let me know if they want anything.'

In the after-cabin the owner's wife stirred in her sleep but did not wake up.

As the motorboat came near the yacht, it reduced speed and the noise of its engines died down to a whisper. With its engines just turning over it glided up astern and a man in a yachting cap and blue-striped cotton jersey put his head out from the control cabin and called.

'Ahoy . . . Ahoy . . . We've got a message for you.'

There were three other men standing at the rail of the launch, athletic-looking figures, two of them wearing dark glasses and with something slung under their armpits. The launch slid up on the windward side of the yacht, its fenders already out. As it came smoothly and expertly alongside with a slight 'gr-gr-gr' of the engines going in reverse, the men swung over the rail without a word and came aboard the yacht.

They acted as if to a prearranged plan,

and the message they had for the yacht was a message of death. They moved fast and surely as if they knew the layout of the yacht and who would be on board. And in fact the yacht had been 'cased' when it was in port in Bermuda. One of them came to the girl and stood over her, pushing her down lightly on to the seat in the cockpit, but with a hand as heavy as a sledge-hammer.

'Just keep still, babe,' he said, 'and you won't get hurt.' The girl stayed there passively, placidly almost, her head in her hands, her eyes closed as if to shut out any consciousness of what was happening. Was she an accessory? Was she?

At the same time the two other men moved independently, spying out the owner and his wife, going one to the main, the other to the after-cabin. Each of them as he got down into the cabin took out a heavy gun he was carrying in a holster under his arm. They were captive-bolt pistols, the humane killers used to fell oxen in slaughter houses. No broken cabin windows, no gaping wounds, no loud reports, little blood even. And yet at close quarters they were as quick and deadly as the most powerful revolver.

The owner moved, but too late.

'What the hell!' he cried, starting up and trying to struggle out of the cramped quarters where he was lying. But the stranger was already beside his bunk, the dark-spectacled face was close above his; one fierce hand on his neck slammed his head against the side of the boat while the other pressed the ready-cocked gun against the side of his head and pulled the trigger. There was a slight explosion, no louder than an air-pistol, and the owner collapsed on the bunk, a little blood welling from the small hole above his ear, a hole made by the steel bolt driven three inches into his brain.

His wife in the after-cabin died even more easily in her sleep, lying on her back, the hole in her sun-browned forehead looking like a red caste mark.

With the same planned energy the two men proceeded to dump the bodies. Stowing their guns, they tore sheets off the bunks and wrapped them round the heads of their two victims so that no mark of bloodstains would be left. Then they went back to the motorboat which was ticking over, moving with the yacht, and held to it by the man who had been at the controls, and now stood at the rail with a boathook. There they picked two 10-pound market-weights with lengths of shock-cord ready wrapped round their handles. Carrying these back to the yacht they dragged the anonymous muffled corpses out on to the deck, wrapped the shock-cords tightly round their necks, hooked the bodies together, then bundled them overboard. For a moment they lay cradled in the light swell and surge round the yacht, then with a swirl of the sheets round their heads, the weights dragged them down into the depths. They were gone out of human knowledge, deep buried in a thousand fathoms of ocean.

The killers turned back to the motorboat and began to transfer to the yacht four boxes that had been left ready waiting in the motorboat's cockpit. They left them stacked side by side on a seat opposite the girl who sat there still with her head in her hands.

'OK,' one of them called to the man at the rail. 'She's all ready. You want us to stow the dope below?'

'No. We'll do that. We have to hide it well. You did a good job boys. Ken will look after you as per contract.' The man gave the boathook to one of the murderers and going to the cabin of the motorboat called to someone inside:

'Come on. Let's get on board.'

He took the kitbag that was handed out to him and boarded the yacht. A woman dressed in a blue jersey and slacks came out of the cabin carrying a small dressing case and followed him across. The three other men were by now back aboard the motorboat. One at the helm revved up the engine, turned the craft away from the yacht and swung round in the direction they had come, soon planing at full speed on a south-westerly course. The whole operation had taken some twenty minutes.

The two newcomers on the yacht began to settle down. They were an

10

athletic-looking couple, a little younger than the two owners who had just been killed, but at first glance not unlike them. They wore dark glasses and yachting gear. The woman went into the after-cabin. The man threw his kitbag down on to the owner's bunk, then spoke to the girl who was still hiding her head in her hands as she sat not moving in the cockpit.

'You're with us now duckie. We'll look after you. You'll have to wait for your boyfriend, but we'll see if we can't fill the gap. We're in for a good cruise. Too bad about the other two. Why don't you go and lie down and get over the shock? I'll stay on watch. Eva can get you a pill. You need a rest and some good dreams.'

'Yes . . . I . . . yes.'

Her voice was flat and dull and she got up and went to one of the forward bunks, moving as if a little drugged already. She lay there but with eyes open.

'It'll be all right . . . all right . . . all right,' she repeated under her breath.

The man moved round the yacht which was now under way, checking the position on the chart and the course on the compass and looking at the log. He slightly eased the mainsheet to catch the wind that had begun to draw aft and adjusted the self-steering. Then he turned to the cases in the cockpit . . .

2

The Virgin Islands

In the crowded anchorage of Long Bay in St Thomas's harbour two yachts were anchored within a short distance of one another just far enough apart to let each of them swing with the wind and the tide. One was a rangy converted 12-metre, flying the Stars-and-Stripes, the other a heavier ketch-rigged cruiser with a centre cockpit and flying the Red Ensign from a short flagpole at the stern.

Rowing from the British to the American boat in a small rubber dinghy, was a middle-aged Englishman in glasses, friendly false teeth and rather baggy khaki shorts. Touches of elegance were added by a blue T-shirt with *Milady*, the name of his yacht, sailing across his chest and a new-looking yachting cap. As he came up behind the Stars-and-Stripes he hailed the 12-metre that gloried in the name of *Yakaboo*.

'Ahoy! *Yakaboo!*'

A short, sunburned girl with her hair in a ponytail, wearing brief shorts and a halter bra tied round her neck and waist, poked her head out and then came on deck.

'Hi,' she said. 'Give me an oar.'

She pulled the dinghy, that had missed the yacht by a good foot, in alongside.

'I'm Linda. What can we do for you?'

'I'm Eric Glazer,' said the man in the dinghy. 'I came over on a scrounging visit I'm afraid. It's breakfast time and we seem to have run out of sugar. My wife Greta won't drink coffee without it and (he waved his hand) it's quite a way ashore even if the shops are open.'

'Sure. You're welcome. Come aboard. Have you got a crock?'

'Well — just this plastic container.'

'Great. Tupperware.'

'I say, this looks a fast boat.'

'Right. It's real fast. She's a converted 35-foot racer. We've just got her on a bare-boat charter.'

'What's that?'

'It means we sail her ourselves. No professional crew. Pop wasn't so keen on that. I guess he'd have liked to make up to a hired lady skipper. But Bella and I persuaded him. Not that Bella wouldn't go for a square-built charter skipper herself.'

'How many do you need to handle her?'

'There's Poppa and a sailing friend and my sister Bella and me. They're all ashore still. We went on the town last night, the last night of our cruise. Bella and I should have been back to sleep on board but Bella's disappeared.'

'Disappeared?'

'Oh, not to worry. She fell into the arms of a dark, handsome Latin lover. Second name Che Valentino. Poppa will be wild about it, but then he and Dene are off on their own private beat up. There, is that enough?' She handed back the container with the sugar in it.

'Heaps thanks. I say, would you and your family like to come over for lunch? That is, if they — I mean if you'd all like to. We've got steaks in the fridge — that is the icebox.'

'Say, that's real kind of you. I guess we'd like to. Have you come over from England?'

'Yes. I've got six months off work and we had a good boat for the crossing. She's a slow old tub, but she got us here all right. We've come up from English Harbour. Made our landfall on Antigua.'

'We picked up our boat in Virgin Gorda and we're ending our cruise here. This place is pretty ugly. The harbour's like dishwater, and the tourists pour in every day from cruise ships and crowd the shops four-deep to buy discount liquor and no-tax luxury goods.'

'Yes we found that out. We're not staying long.'

'I expect we've both been able to visit some beautiful solitary places. We found the British Virgins great. But the Chesapeake's good too. You ought to sail up there.'

'I expect we will too. Before we go back across. See you all for lunch anyway, I hope.'

'Nice girl,' thought Eric Glazer as he rowed back to his boat and left Linda wondering what had happened to the others. She was a girl who was ready to make friends and think the best of people. Unlike her sister Bella she was not a classical beauty, but her wide eyes, generous mouth and snub nose added up to something attractive — whether she was being serious over some problem or bubbling with fun and enthusiasm.

★ ★ ★

Over an hour after Eric Glazer had visited *Yakaboo*, getting on for ten, a battered motorboat, one of the harbour taxis, came out to the yacht at a sober pace; though sober was the last word to describe its passengers. Linda had put out a welcoming head, but narrowed her eyes when she saw the occupants. Drew and Dene were returning with a couple of floozies in tow.

Ten days earlier Drew, Bella, Linda and Dene had flown from Baltimore and picked up their boat in Virgin Gorda. The oldest of the party, Drew Campbell, was a senior member of the Matapeake Sailing Club and a realtor from Baltimore. Drew was medium height and heavily built, a good 15-stone with a tendency to stoutness. He had the heavy shoulders and stocky neck of a football player, blunt features and hale, sunburned complexion. His bluff manner and forthright views ensured him a hearing in most male sailing circles. Drew's friend, the other member of the party, Dene Stevens, sailing secretary of the same yacht club, was an experienced hand at cruising in the West Indies and he and Drew had been friends for years.

Drew's two girls, Bella and Linda, had grown up sailing from their childhood. Bella, the elder one, had been to finishing school and university in Europe and this sailing holiday was a sort of celebration for her return home. She had come back a beauty. The perfect oval of her face was complemented by clearly arched eyebrows, a classical nose and a fine complexion. She not only had good features and a good figure, she followed her mother in looking *soignée* even at her most *sportif*.

Drew's wife, Paula was not on the cruise. In her opinion sailing was for children and morons, but she had agreed to fly down at the end of the cruise to join them for a day's shopping in Charlotte Amalie, St Thomas.

The cruise had gone well. The boat was fast and easily handled. They had kept themselves in fresh fish and the weather hadn't blown up. There had been some family ribbing, but all had been well between them on the surface except for one big row between Drew and Bella. Drew, against instructions ('Don't throw it Poppa.'), had carelessly tossed a favourite compact of Bella's overboard into the sea. She had called her father a blue-arsed baboon and they had both lost their tempers.

For most of the holiday they had lived on the boat so when they got into Charlotte Amalie harbour early the previous afternoon, they were all ready for a party ashore. Especially as, according to Dene, the town offered the full treatment: casinos with French croupiers, Japanese saunas, a genuine Russian émigré restaurant where it took three waiters to bring in the hors d'oeuvres, topless bars by the bosomful, discotheques, allnite nude cabarets — and everything, again according to Dene, with a real local flavour.

'We'll paint her redder than red,' Drew promised. 'You girls can do a Cinderella act at midnight and we fellers will make a night of it.'

'I'm not mad to go ashore,' said Linda.

She wasn't one to pour cold water on projects for outings, but she wanted to think about her new friend Martin. He was a visitor to the Matapeake Yacht Club and he seemed to have fallen for her in a big way. Besides sailing together he had taken her out on the town a couple of times and they had got on as though it was Thanksgiving and Christmas rolled together. If it went on, the inevitable result would be that they would end up in each other's arms.

'Trouble is he's English,' she told

Bella. 'Poppa's funny about the English. Sometimes he gets on with them, but he's inclined to think they're a la-di-da lot. Sure, Martin isn't like that. He's in one of the most practical businesses there is — insurance. And can he handle a boat, it's magic. He's got a sixth sense for wind and tides and a butterfly touch on the tiller.'

'Poppa talks a lot of hot air,' said Bella. 'He's full of these prejudices. But once he meets him he'll come round. I'm the one he thinks goes over the top. I want to go out tonight. I'm bored. I haven't had a man friend for ages. I might meet a real thrill in a sophisticated place like this. Come on — do come along. I don't want to go on my own.'

'All right, I'll join you then.'

Linda spoke more loudly to include Drew and Dene, who had just joined them, in what she said.

'I'll come with you if someone will stand treat for a super supper — something with five courses that melt in your mouth.'

'We'll go to the *Escargot*,' Dene decided. 'The food's out of this world.'

* * *

Around midnight they were in a topless bar and discotheque called *The Village Virgin*. Dene was chatting to a dark girl who had just done a cabaret number while Drew was being pushed round the floor by a mauve-blonde taxi-dancer sheathed in black.

While the men were thus preoccupied the girls were left with drinks at a table. Linda was waving at a waiter to get her a taxi while Bella, bored, only one dance with a clumsy American boy to her credit, was in half a mind to join her.

But fate lay in wait. A tall, good-looking stranger at a table near the back of the room had been looking at the girls for some time — though he was also deep in conversation with two other men. All three were prosperous-looking and they were discussing business in a mixture of English and Spanish. The man interested in the girls was a visitor.

The other two were locals very much at home in Charlotte Amalie.

'*He! Por ahí*,' said the visitor. 'See those bimbos sitting by themselves. Those two outdoor types. Classy American girls for sure. I could be interested in the older one. She looks sophisticated and bored with things.'

'We get American women visiting here all the time,' said one of the locals. 'A lot of them are on the look out for a man.'

'I need a smart girl in the firm, since we just lost a good operator. Perhaps we could train this one for the job. Think you could get me an introduction?'

'Sure.'

'I might combine business and pleasure. There's nothing like . . . er pleasure . . . to get the *signoras* attached to you.'

'No harm in trying. We'll make it part of the deal we're discussing. A discount thrown in — eh! Juan, you know the manager of this joint. Get him to come over.'

★ ★ ★

'Our friend here, Monsieur Ramón Aragón, an important Venezuelan visitor, would like to meet one of those two young ladies over there,' Juan explained to the manager. 'Could you ask politely for us please.'

The manager nodded and went over to the girls' table.

'Sure,' said Bella to the manager's bowed invitation. 'Wheel him over. I can take Venezuelans with tabasco in my soup.'

'Are you all right? Want me to stay?' Linda asked.

'You go back to the boat and dream of Martin, honey. After all, Poppa's around even though he is glassy-eyed. And it's America here — America the golden, with milk and hashish blessed. Those dagos are mostly big eyes and soulful sighs. I can keep my end up and if I can't I can always surrender gracefully. That finishing place taught us to be graceful in all we do.'

So while Bella met her rich sporty Ramón, Linda got her taxi to the Yacht Club and rowed herself out to the yacht in the dinghy. In the velvet black tropical night the full moon hung among the stars like a silver penny. After the feverish disco the night air was cool and caressing and Linda lay on her bunk and thought of Martin until she dropped off to sleep.

★ ★ ★

Now, in mid-morning, Dene and Drew — two bad cases of the morning after — were approaching the yacht. With them still were their partners of the previous evening. Somewhere, somehow, the women had changed into day clothes, but the men were crumpled, bug-eyed and had croaking voices.

'Hi, Linda, honey,' Drew came alongside with determined bonhomie. 'We just brought the girls out for a last snifter. We had us a party, eh Dene. Is that town redder than a soldier's coat! Lindy, this is Dolores (waving a hand at the dark girl). Come on sugar, here's a hand on board *Yakaboo*.'

'How do, *Buenos días!*' Dolores smiled.

'And this is Carolina — in the morning.'

'What a dandy little runabout,' chirruped Carolina. 'My, how do you know what to pull with all those different ropes? I'd sure get tangled up in this craft.'

'That's knowing the ropes, honey,' croaked Drew. 'Like you sure know the ropes in your own craft.'

Carolina giggled and gave Drew a playful nudge.

Dene paid off the water-taxi when they had all climbed on board. Drew at once took charge of the bar, handing out drinks in plastic tumblers which were decorated with lightly-clad girls.

'Where's Bella?' he asked suddenly. 'She came back with you last night — didn't she?'

'I thought you would be looking after her when I left,' Linda answered. 'I came back on my ownsome lonesome. Under plush Caribbean skies alone.'

'Huh. Then where the jumping jiminy is she, the young tramp? We're handing the yacht back tomorrow and you girls are flying home to Baltimore. And your

26

mother'll be here this evening. It's a good time for her to do a bunk, the little hobo — where is she?'

'If I know anything about it she's following in father's footsteps,' said Linda very coolly. 'Having a night out with a local visitor — a rich Venezuelan. She can look after herself.'

'Dene, we'd better get these bints ashore. Can you take them in the dinghy? Now what's this about a Venezuelan? I'm not having any dago laying my girls. She'd better know that.'

'Wow! Here she is,' Linda pointed. 'Looks as if she's hooked herself a conquistador.'

The craft that came surging across the water might have been the state barge of royalty, all teak and chromium and powered by superb engines. The passengers sat, embowered in leather and cushions in a centre cockpit. The coxswain was in a plastic dome further forward, another sailor stood in a smaller cockpit in the stern. It circled the yacht setting it rocking, not over gently, and almost swamped Dene and his women passengers on their way ashore in the yacht's small dinghy.

Then as the helmsman throttled down, its rearing bow dropped to the water and it crept alongside *Yakaboo* purring like a cat full of cream, and almost matching the yacht in length and breadth. At bow and stern the two crew threw over fenders and held the launch alongside with boathooks.

'Hi! Good morning all.' Bella still wearing the matching jeans, blouson and headscarf of the previous evening, was in high spirits.

'And not before time. Where have you been?' bellowed Drew.

Another voice broke in: 'Señor Campbell, sir. May I introduce myself. Your charming daughter here has done the honour to be shown round and breakfast in my friend's country house.' The dark, handsome man beside Bella bowed and spread his hands in a showy, respectful gesture, standing up in the cockpit. 'I am Ramón Aragón. I represent Caribbean Traders — international trading but with interest in pharmaceuticals too.'

'Poppa, it was fabulous. We went water-skiing before breakfast. Now come for a ride in the launch, you and Linda. Come on Linda.'

'Damned if I will, lousy Latin,' Drew muttered.

But he let himself be persuaded, and he and the two girls sank into the luxury of the large cockpit while Ramón made up a low table and produced ice-cold Martinis from a cocktail cabinet. When they had their drinks he said something to the cox and the barge with a roar of engines skimmed across the harbour and circled a great white cruise ship that was moving slowly in to dock. Then like a bird they flew over the waves to the harbour entrance, returning at full speed until they were within a few yards of *Yakaboo*. She stopped planing, the bow dropped and she floated alongside to let them get back aboard.

Ramón, with a last flowery speech and going as dramatically as he had come, sped back to the shore. Again he nearly swamped Dene, this time on his way back to the yacht.

'Now then, what the hell do you mean going off with that — that — ' Drew turned on Bella as soon as they were alone.

'Poppa, he's fabulously rich and so are his friends. He's a super swimmer — and he's fun to be with. He's in some international business. And he's promised he'll look us up in Baltimore. I hope he does.'

'All right, all right — you're leaving on the plane tomorrow,' Drew growled.

'And he's got the best line in hash I ever tried,' Bella said defiantly.

'Bella, look out. Don't get hooked on drugs,' Linda heard herself being preachy though it wasn't what she meant.

'You're both going on that plane. That's final,' shouted Drew.

'Don't shout, Poppa. What's for lunch?' Bella said calmly.

'There isn't anything,' Linda confessed. 'But we've been asked to lunch by the boat next door,' she pointed. 'That yacht *Milady*. They're English. He came over to borrow some sugar.'

'Limey's eh. Well that's better than Venezuelans. After lunch, Linda, you can come out to the airport with me to meet your Ma. She's arriving half after five. We'll check into the hotel then come back and get the boat ready for handover. There are some items on the inventory missing.'

3

Piracy Up-to-date

The following is an extract from an article which appeared in the *Monthly Yacht Magazine*:

'In yachting circles, when discussion turns to long-distance cruising, the question of safety at sea is one that arouses immediate interest. Every sport has its risks, and a spice of adventure adds zest to the blue-gold days at sea and the getaway-from-it-all atmosphere of an ocean cruise. When it is a question of the boat, the gear, the supplies, the ability to navigate, to organise the crew and ensure good relations on board — then the yachtsman has, or should have, control of the situation. Short of a freak storm or an uncharted reef, there should be no more risk of serious accident in a well-organised sailing venture than in any other sport or recreation.

'Unfortunately in recent years, it seems there is the possibility of another hazard which is not so easily guarded against. It used to be called piracy; now yachtsmen give it the name of yacht-jacking or hijacking. The evidence in the nature of the case is largely circumstantial. But in the States there are indications and a strong body of opinion, to the effect that the hundreds of yacht disappearances which occur there, are by no means all due to the natural hazards of storm and shipwreck. US Coastguard files show that over 600 boats have vanished in mysterious circumstances and in good weather, and they even took the step of issuing a warning notice: 'Yachtsmen planning to set out for a cruise . . . should be aware that their yachts may become a target for a modern-day pirate or hijacker . . . '

'The nub of the problem is the lack of information and hard evidence. If yacht-jacking is properly done there is no one left to tell the tale. In the words of a Congressional investigator it is 'the closest thing to a perfect crime you can have.' Almost the only case that has been clearly established is that of the *Kamilili* in which the hijackers put the crew over the side two days out of Honolulu, but made the mistake of giving them a rubber life-raft. The crew were picked up five days later, the yacht was tracked down in an air-sea operation, and the pirates arrested. If they had murdered the crew, they would never have been caught.

'It may seem 'old hat' now to talk about the Bermuda Triangle, but there have been far more unexplained disappearences in this area and on the Florida coast than elsewhere. One reason must be the enormous number of pleasure boats in these waters, not only local craft, but yachts from the West Coast, from Europe, South Africa and the Mediterranean, on trans-Atlantic or round-the-world voyages. A second factor is that the drug traffic operates on a big scale in the West Indies and South America, and there may be a connection between yacht-jacking and the drug trade. Both crimes are made easier by the fact that the West Indies and South America are a patchwork of independent countries, many of them racket-ridden with little will or ability for law-enforcement. Drug-runners and hijackers can move from one territory to another to avoid detection or capture, and efficient surveillance and investigation of missing yachts is virtually impossible.

'Among the countries of Western Europe there is better coordination, though here too . . .'

4

Visitors

'That was a great meal, Ma'am,' said Drew to Greta Glazer after lunch in Charlotte Amalie harbour. 'You folk from the old country sure know how to make yourselves comfortable on a boat.'

'Only by copying you Americans — ice for instance. In England you can't buy ice for boats everywhere as you can here.'

'Well we've been mighty interested to see your boat. And I want you both to come and visit with us in Baltimore. Come ashore for a piece. My wife Paula'll be tickled to show you her collection of enamels — some of her best pieces are English — a Henry Ffoukes snuff-box dating, when? Bella you're the expert.'

'It's about 1790. But Poppa, the Glazers may not be interested.'

'Oh yes, we'd be interested all right.

A collection like that. But we're not experts.'

'I'll give you the phone number and the house location. Make it in a month and it'll be Regatta time. You can be guests of the Yacht Club and get in on the racing scene.'

'That's very kind of you. We'd love to. We'll phone up when we get to the Chesapeake Bay area.'

'That's the ticket.'

★ ★ ★

The Campbell home in Baltimore was a fine southern Colonial-style mansion set in a roomy garden in one of the older suburbs. Late on Wednesday afternoon the two girls, a few weeks back from their cruise, were hitting tennis-balls at one another while Paula, in the drawing-room, had just ordered tea out near the tennis-court. An expensive car came up the drive and a stranger, elegant in flannels and a blazer, got out and came to the door.

'He's a foreign gentleman,' announced

Dinah, the house maid. 'He asked for Missy Bella. He said they met each other in the Virgin Islands.'

'Oh, that must be the English couple Drew asked to stay. Ask him to come in.'

But the tall, dark visitor was not English.

'Señora Campbell, you are Bella's mother?'

'That's right.'

'I am honoured to meet you. I introduce myself — Ramón Aragón from Caracas. I met your charming daughter in Saint Thomas.'

'Oh yes. They were down in the Virgin Islands sailing with their father and a friend. I flew down for a day's shopping. Drew didn't mention about you.'

'I met with your husband too. I was not sure then that I would be in Baltimore.'

'You asked for Bella?'

'Your most charming daughter. Now I can see where she gets her great beauty.'

'The girls are out playing tennis. We'll go and find them.'

38

'What a charming mansion,' Ramón waved his arms expansively. 'And furniture of choice antique.'

'Yes, I look after the house. We've got some good bits of early furniture.'

'I drove up from Miami in my Rolls car. I have business in New York, but I wanted to stop for a break and Bella invited me to see your Regatta — as a yachtsman you understand.'

'My, you came in a Rolls! Drew wanted one, but he says he can't afford it — not while I keep collecting nice things for the house.'

'They are nice cars to drive.'

'You must stay for tea. They're all going down to the cottage to prepare for the Regatta.'

'Down to the sea?'

'We have a country place near the Yacht Club. Maybe you could go down with them. They'll be sailing some. I expect you could stay at the cottage if you want.'

'That is indeed gracious. I have a flat in town, but the cottage would be delightful.'

'Come out and meet them. We'll have tea outside.'

★ ★ ★

'Hi! It's Ray for goodness sake! Goody.'

Exercise had given Bella a slightly dishevelled appearance that enhanced her beauty. Linda, plainer, just looked damp and flushed, but she still had her youthful attractiveness.

'Mr Aragón is staying for tea.'

'Oh please call me Ramón.'

'He could go down to the cottage with you girls and Martin for the weekend. There's plenty of room.'

'Poppa *will* be pleased,' Linda remarked in an undertone to her mother.

'Drew should realise the obligations of hospitality. If he invites people up here he should look after them,' Mrs Campbell replied.

'He didn't, Mom — it was that English couple he invited, the Glazers.'

At that moment footsteps crunched on the gravel.

'Good afternoon Mrs Campbell. Hullo

Linda, Bella. Sorry I'm late.'

It was Martin, dressed for sailing, who had parked his car in front of the house and walked round to the sound of voices.

'I was kept at the office. Too many boats want insurance — and everything's urgent.'

'Hullo Martin,' Paula greeted him. 'You don't know Señor Ramón Aragón. He's another yachtsman and another visitor to this part of the world. Martin Firth is seconded from England to a local insurance firm,' she explained to Ramón. 'It's the company I insure my valuables with.'

'How do you do,' said Martin. 'Is that your elegant machine out front — the Rolls?'

'Are you coming down with us, Mom?' asked Linda.

'No dear. I've got a man coming to look at my collection. I might put in an appearance at the Regatta itself.'

'Mom's collection is famous, Ray,' Bella explained. 'You ought to see it some time. It's worth goodness knows how much.'

'So Madame Campbell, besides your beautiful furniture you have another collection?'

'Yes, they are small *objets d'art* — decorated snuff boxes and other small enamels. I chose them all myself.'

'Ah Madame Campbell, it is clear you have collector's flair. It goes with a true artistic sense. You are a guardian of the world's cultural heritage.'

'It's gallant of you to say so — Ramón. Some time you must see my collection. And I'd love a spin in that swell automobile of yours.'

'It will be a pleasure.'

'Now here's the tea. I know you're all crazy to get out on the water, but you've time for tea. Martin will tell you how important it is in England.'

★ ★ ★

Bella drove off with Ramón for the cottage on Crab Alley in expensive luxury, while Linda travelled with Martin in his modest Ford roadster.

'That was a surprise,' said Linda.

'Bella's wild oats coming home to roost.'

'To be nipped in the bud by your father and, er — be swept under the carpet and vanish like smoke, don't you think?'

'No seriously Martin, I'm not so sure. Bella played it icecool with me and said she couldn't care less about Ramón. But he's good-looking, rich and dashing. You saw how pleased she was when he turned up. Bella's bored with being at home and Poppa's heavy hand might make her do the other thing. It's her idea of romance — adventure, living dangerously. Ramón's sure a charmer too. Didn't Mom fall for the dear man. She'd take him on herself if she didn't have all her art critics.'

'Well, we'll just have to wait and see. But Ramón's not my favourite buddy even on five minutes acquaintance. At least your father doesn't object to me even though I am a Limey.'

'Darling how could he?' Linda brushed a feather of a kiss on to Martin's cheek. Martin sighed and tried to concentrate on the road ahead.

They drove out through downtown Baltimore. In sixteen miles they came to the Chesapeake Bay bridges, then south on to smaller roads, over bayous, through farmland and eventually into scrub and marsh. In an hour they had covered the thirty miles to Cox Neck. Finally with a crackling of gravel under the tyres they ran up the drive to the Crab Creek cottage, where Ramón's car was already parked in front of the porch. At the moment there were just the four of them. Drew would not get out until early Saturday. But in the meantime they would drive over to Matapeake to the Yacht Club and practise for the Regatta.

5

Nightmare

The room was one of a number in a cheap tenement block in a poor district, situated up a narrow staircase and at the back of the building. They were all cheap furnished apartments where the rent was paid weekly in advance and no questions asked. There was a single bed against one wall; across a corner was a curtain with hooks behind it where a few clothes could be hung. Next to it was a cheap dresser and a square of mirror with the silver worn round the edges. The sole provision for cooking and meals was a gas-ring on a kitchen table. A strip of faded carpet, a wash-basin and a curtain over the window completed the furnishings.

The young woman on the bed was ill. She was suffering from acute drug withdrawal symptoms and as she was on the run there was no one she could call for help. For some years she had been working for a drug syndicate. She was a carrier. Her role was to be respectable-looking, secure, well-spoken, to travel comfortably and stay in the best places. She would pick up a packet, a book, a piece of luggage, a picture, an antique. She would pick it up at one place and deliver it discreetly at another — sometimes in the same country, sometimes from country to country. She travelled in Europe and America, spoke English and fair French, was educated and well-groomed. She did what she was told and she was very well paid.

At first the work had gone well. Then she started taking drugs herself. They gave her a lift when she was with a friend or a lover and soothed her when she was alone. Gradually they became more necessary and the doses increased. They began to affect her appearance and her performance. She received a warning just as she received all her delivery instructions — by telephone.

Then one day she had been returning

from Bermuda and flying to Washington with a duty-free bottle of whiskey and a carton of 200 'special' cigarettes in her luggage. Somehow she had left the cigarettes in a cab on the way from the airport to her hotel. They were not returned despite frantic telephone calls to the cab company. She was also unable to trace the driver. She had gone into the shop where she was to leave the cigarettes and reported the loss.

'That's bad,' said the shopkeeper, a sandy-haired, middle-aged man with pale blue eyes. 'That's bad, honey. They won't be pleased, they won't be pleased at all. This isn't the first time something's gone wrong, is it now?'

Then she had panicked. If the cab-driver had decided to retire on the proceeds of the cigarettes and sold them to a rival mob — that wasn't funny. But it would be worse if they were handed in to the police and the police traced her. The firm might decide she was too much of a danger. After all, she could inform on the location of dozens of dealers and handlers. And she could easily be eliminated — made safe.

So she checked out of her expensive hotel and took a cheap furnished apartment downtown, hoping that, cut off from her usual contacts, she could lie low. For a time the money held out and she got by on drugs with the aid of a pusher who hung round the bars and had a soft spot for her. But the cost ate up her funds and even he wouldn't supply her for nothing.

Now, after three days without drugs, she was drowned deep in agony. The ants were the worst. Chrissake those crawling armies! Ants seen in close-up, standing over her with steel legs, heads in armoured helmets, shield-like eyes and torpedo bodies. Behind the leaders were millions more, spreading over the floor, the walls, the ceiling. She was shut in with them! No escape! If she shut her eyes she could feel them on her skin. If she brushed them off they would crawl underneath . . . under her skin . . . in her flesh . . . they would eat away her body. She arched her back in the bed. A half-scream forced her lips apart. Then at an order from the master robot the ranks halted, thinned, melted away. She opened her eyes to the blotched ceiling, the stained walls, the threadbare carpet. Trembling she dragged herself to the basin, dabbed her moist forehead and tried to pour a few drops from an empty whiskey bottle into an empty glass.

There were other nightmares almost as bad. There were the snakes . . . cold, sinuous worms with scabby coils, flickering tongues and fetid kisses that came in the dark. Round her neck and chest they would tighten until she could hardly breathe . . . if she could break free . . . then she would manage to twist in bed and reach the light switch. They were gone — but they would come again. For a time she held out, but what was there to hold out *for*? It would go on. It would get worse. The dread of something worse haunted her . . .

There was enough money in her bag for sleeping pills and a bottle of bourbon to wash them down. With red-rimmed eyes and shaking hands she got on a pair of shoes and went shopping. When she got back she put the bottles on the dresser and looked at them — one big, one small. She took a slug of the bourbon. The warmth ran down her throat and spread to her stomach. Then she swallowed half-a-dozen pills . . . half-a-dozen more . . . washed them down with liquor . . . then more pills. Unsteadily she put the whiskey bottle on the dresser and made for the bed. But dark clouds came rushing into her head and she collapsed before she got there.

For some hours she lay, her breathing short and throaty, her face and body heavy with sweat. Then she vomited a little, and choked as some of it was breathed into her lungs. Her breathing grew more painful, but she neither woke nor stirred — then her breathing stopped.

She might have lain there until the rent was due in a week's time, but it was the next day that a car stopped at the apartments and two men got out. The front door of the building was locked and there was a row of push-buttons with names of tenants by the side of the heavy door. The men seemed to have prior information for they rang a bell with no name against it. There was no reply, but they rang repeatedly and waited and after a few minutes they were let in by a woman who happened to be coming out from another apartment. They marched upstairs and knocked at the number they were looking for. One of them called out, 'Come on gorgeous. Open up.' But no one answered.

When again there was no reply the first man nodded to the heavyweight who was with him. The second man put his shoulder to the door and broke it open as if it belonged to a doll's house. The flimsy lock gave easily and no one in nearby rooms apparently heard the sound of it.

'She's stiff,' said the first man as he turned the body over, lifted the arm and let it thud back on to the floor. He sniffed at the whiskey bottle and looked critically at the label on the bottle of pills.

'It's tough when you're hooked and haven't got it. Anyway she's saved us a job.'

They lifted the body and put it on

the bed under the bedclothes. They went through her bag and her case removing any papers or means of identification. They went through the clothes in drawers and on hangers removing any tags. They left the bottle of bourbon and the near-empty bottle of pills.

'That's the lot then boss,' said the heavyweight.

'Yes. And now we have to recruit another dame. A good-looking American girl like this one would be just right.'

6

Romance

When Bella and Ramón went out for a sail in Bella's Hobie Cat, Linda and Martin took the opportunity to go for a walk among the flats of Crab Alley with their bathing suits.

'I love this place,' said Linda. 'There are miles of rivers and creeks to sail. You can drop a hook almost anywhere and be in a cosy anchorage, then fish in the eel holes — with hardly a rock or ledge to worry about. Rivers ramble up to fifty miles past old landings where they shipped tobacco, cotton and rice to England in the old days. There's history everywhere. I'd never want to leave it.'

'I was going to ask if you would leave it,' said Martin, 'at least leave it for a bit. The firm wants me to go back to England. How about coming back with me — as Mrs Firth?'

'You mean you want to make me a respectable married woman?'

'That's what I mean, Linda darling. How about it? We get on ashore and afloat, in bed and out of it. Paula likes me and even Drew has made friendly noises since he knew I've got a respectable job and can sail a boat. My family would fall head over heels for you. Anyhow it's us that counts.'

'Yes, it's us that counts. I don't know anyone I'd rather be with. But you mean I'd have to give up all this? Just think, you can sail through waterways here with salt marshes on either side, and just herons, gulls and snipe for company, with clams and oysters everywhere and miles of sheltered water.'

'You mightn't have to give it up for good. I've got the prospect of a permanent job here in a year or two. Meanwhile we've got some pretty lonely sailing in England from the Scilly Isles and the Helford River to the little creeks and anchorages on the north side of the Isle of Wight. If you want something really remote there are always the Hebrides. For that matter you can be secluded in a boat almost anywhere.'

'Seclusion's fine with me, provided it's me alone with you — alone with me.'

'Besides I love you — on a boat or off it.' Martin put his arms round her and gave her a bear-hug of a kiss.

'Darling you've convinced me. Maybe I'm not too hard to persuade. England'll be fine.'

'Darling.'

'Darling.'

Their conversation was interrupted by more important things. The herons and even the oysters were temporarily forgotten.

Linda was the first to recover. 'Let's keep it to ourselves for the time being,' she said. Time enough to tell the family when you have to go back to England.'

'That's all right by me.'

'Gosh when I think what it will mean. I've never been out of this country for a start. I'm not the cosmopolitan Bella is — Switzerland and France are nothing new to her.'

'You'll like England. As I've said, there's good sailing in summer though you have to give up in winter. It's the cold and the short days. It doesn't get any rougher weather in winter and you don't get hurricanes like you get here. But there's plenty of other things to do and see — stately homes, churches, museums.

'Yes, Mom's keen on all that.'

'There's always country walking too. You don't get he-man trails like some places here, but cosy villages, woods and hills with a pub for lunch like as not.'

'What's a pub?'

'Come and find out. It's the nearest we get to conviviality. The best pubs can be ideal places to enjoy a drink or a chat or local food, the worst can be ear-shattering dumps to get drunk in as noisily as possible.'

'I'll wait and see,' said Linda. 'I guess the range sounds to be about the same as here. You can find noise and drink around here, and drugs too for that matter.'

'Drugs eh. That's something I don't go for.'

'Nor me. But I wouldn't say the same about Bella.' Linda frowned. 'I'm really worried about her, Martin. I'm with you and Poppa in not liking this flashy Ray she's cultivating. She's a bit hypnotised by his money and the handsome-stranger angle. She seems to think he's the most glamorous thing that ever walked round in men's trousers.'

'He won't be here for ever, as I said. She'll get over it.'

'I hope so. Something that might crop up is a berth on the Glazers' boat. They came over alone, just the two of them. But they found it heavy work keeping watches all the time. They thought of trying to get someone to crew on the way back. If Poppa got talking to Eric Glazer he might arrange for Bella to go and have a holiday in England.'

'You'd be the ideal crew, Linda. But then I couldn't do without you all that time. You said the boat didn't look too fast so the crossing could take five weeks or more.'

'I enjoy sailing with you too much to go with anyone else. Anyway we've got to get this Regatta over first. You're hoping to go in for the Hobie Cat race, aren't you?'

'I think I might have a fair chance. Your father's given a trophy, hasn't he? There is a spare boat going at the Club and I've got keen on multihulls since I've been over here.'

'Bella's got her own Hobie Cat. Dad gave us both one, but I used mine in part-payment for the two-berth cruiser we've been out in. I think Ramón might have an eye on sailing Bella's in the Regatta, if she'll let him.'

'Cats are good boats for racing. They're identical so everyone's equal. And they're not too expensive, so you get a good turnout. Tornadoes are faster but not more exciting.

'Here we are,' Linda announced. 'This is a good place to swim. It's deep but there's no current. And there aren't any spectators so we don't need our costumes.'

'Suits me — or doesn't suit me I should say. When I'm sailing I often go overboard from the yacht in the nude. There's something special about the feel of the water if you aren't covered up. Besides, *you* look smashing in the altogether.'

Their swim was cold but exhilarating. They were both at home in the water. If anything Linda was the better stylist, but Martin almost made up for it by brute strength substituting for gracefulness. In the event it was Linda who was able to rib him mildly when she won both their races.

'Here's to the next time we go sailing or swimming together,' said Linda when they were lying and drying out in the sun.

She held up a plastic cup of Californian-type Liebfraumilch she had brought along as part of their picnic.

★ ★ ★

Martin's next sail was to be in the Hobie Cat race. But their next long sail together was to be very different from what either of them expected. In fact moments of it were to be a matter of life and death for Martin and imminent storm danger for them both.

7

Regatta

The cottage on Crab Alley which the girls shared with Drew had been a small plantation house in the old slave days. It was only fifty yards from a landing-stage where cotton had once been rowed out to clippers waiting at anchor in the deeper channels until they had a full load for the mills of Lancashire in England. The shoal waters round the house were ideal for small boat sailing — they were favoured with moderate tides and except in the hurricane season, were sheltered from strong winds.

From early childhood the girls had enjoyed warm days on the water — or in the water at favourite bathing places. There had been other children to join in and at the Yacht Club, only two miles away on the other side of Kent, there had been junior races in catboats and dinghies. The annual Regatta and other clubs' Regattas were always exciting and meets of the Chesapeake Station of the famous Cruising Club of America never lacked interest. Usually there had been a grown-up ready to take out youngsters who could make themselves useful.

Now Bella, coming back to a childhood playground, rather affected to look down on it all, wanting wider horizons and calling it 'the same old crowd' or 'dull as pumping bilge-water'. For Linda who had been there all along, the place had a heart-warming familiarity. The minus factor for Linda was that it had grown in noise and numbers and glossiness. There were more marinas, more boats, more engines, more transistors, and there was more pollution.

It was only farther off, down on the outer barrier islands protected by the Conservancy, that one could get right away and be really alone except for the birds and the fish and the odd oysterman for company. Her favourite spots now were in the chain of lonely islands that ran along Assawoman, Metomkin and the other Inlets.

But today was special, with flags and racing and champagne to celebrate — and Linda was prepared to enjoy that too, especially as Martin was there to share it with her.

The Matapeake Yacht Club was on the west shore of Kent Island some three miles below the big parallel bridges across the bay to Baltimore on Route 50 — east. Matapeake was very much a private club, but this was their Annual Regatta and the premises and entry to the races was thrown open to the world and there were spectators and racing boats from all over. There were Regattas at nearly a dozen other centres but Matapeake was one of the most popular.

The crowd was growing and the place was bustling with people and boats. The Clubhouse stood on level ground with a lawn round it and neat gravelled paths, flanked at intervals by old iron cannons. At the entrance to the main building were two much finer brass cannons used on occasions for a *feu de joie*. The lawns ran down to the water where vertical stone facing, with a good depth of water up to it, gave easy access to three wooden stages, built out at right angles where boats could go alongside and tie up temporarily. Farther along opposite a crane and a recovery dock there were marina berths with power and water laid on and beyond that again rows of moorings. It was one of thc best fitted out private clubs in the district.

The club flagpole and several boats in the marina were dressed for the occasion with strings of international code flags. The club had erected bleachers in front of the Clubhouse opposite the finishing line, for spectators to sit and watch the races, and they looked like being full.

As an especial honour the *Pride of Baltimore*, a real Baltimore clipper, a perfect reproduction of one of those racing greyhounds of another age, had come across for the Regatta and dropped anchor offshore out of the way of the races. She was most impressive when under sail, but even at anchor, long low and shapely, decked with flags, with her enormous bowsprit, her overhanging mizzen boom and her masts raked back almost to a thirty degree angle, she looked a genuine racing thoroughbred.

Also at anchor but ready for racing later, were four of the famous old log-canoes — yachts with big overhangs, low freeboard like the early 12-metres, and carrying an enormous spread of canvas. They carried big crews and had 'springboards' fitted which, like modern trapezes, enabled the crew to get out to windward to balance the boat when they were thrashing into the wind. The race for the log-canoes would be a feature of the afternoon.

Coming and going at the jetties there were boats of all sizes, loading and unloading passengers and crew. There were Hampton and Indian-Landing one-class designs, Oxford 400s, 8-metre sloops and Class Q sloops. Besides catboats of all sizes there were skipjacks and bugeyes, and even a few clinker-built Seabright skiffs down from the Jersey coast. Steward boats and stewards on shore with loud-hailers would clear away all the spectator craft and non-racing boats well before two-o'clock when the first race began.

★ ★ ★

Standing in front of the Clubhouse at the side of the bleachers were Drew Campbell, his friend Dene Stevens and another man called Scottie to whom Drew was describing their latest cruise.

'The last day of sailing we visited Charlotte Amalie on St Thomas in the Virgins and say, boy, you never met virgins like them, eh Dene!'

'Sure it was quite a visit,' Dene nodded, with a grin. 'You ought to try it, Scottie.'

'It's a free port down there too. Luxury goods from here to Chinatown, enough to beat gay Paree. Bella went wild and even Paula flew down at the end to join in the fun.'

'Drew, we've got more than twenty boats in the Hobie Cat race,' said Dene, half his attention on his secretarial duties. 'I reckon we ought to move the marker buoy farther out from the starting line.'

'That Limey boy, Martin, could arrange it for you. He's been real handy since he joined the club. He's going in the Hobie Cat race.'

'Keep an eye out for him then, will you Drew. We've got time. You're right about the Virgins though. That was a party we had. What was that dancing girl called, Carmen something?'

'Conchita it was. She had plenty of it, not to say tit, if I remember. It was quite a club that Village Virgin.'

'Mr Campbell sir, I am looking for the charming Bella'. Ramón interrupted them. 'She has kindly lent me her little boat to go in for a catamaran race.'

'Did she indeed,' said Drew sourly. 'I gave her that boat.'

'Of course they are just children's toys, not real boats at all. But I have raced catamarans.'

'I'll have you know they are very popular here and give excellent racing.'

Drew spoke with feeling. His interest in boats, like his interest in most things, was not without its business angle. His realtor business took most of his time, but advised by his friend Dene, he had taken the Hobie Cat agency and he had helped promote this race. He had placed the boats with retailers in Maryland, Virginia and part of Delaware — and they were selling like ice-cream in August. You couldn't expect them to replace the Comet, for after all that had been designed right on the spot in Miles river, Chesapeake Bay. The Hobie Cat had been built 2000 miles away in a Quonset hut by the Pacific Ocean in San Juan, Capistrano. But the Hobie Cat was catching up.

'My racing,' said Ramón self-importantly, 'has been with the aristo-cats, with Tornadoes no less. But I expect I can handle these babies too. I aim to win.'

'Do you now,' said Drew. 'Well that's interesting. It happens my money is going on to my young Limey friend. Bella isn't here, if you want to know.'

'In that case I will wish you good day, gentlemen,' Ramón gave a slight, stiff bow with an almost mocking effect in its parody of military precision. Then he strode off.

'What do you know about that,' muttered Drew. 'Damned dago. I hope Martin beats the pants off him. It beats me why Bella's fallen for him. I've got to get her away for a vacation . . . '

'Maybe I shouldn't talk,' said Dene, 'seeing I haven't got any family. But it seems to me you've got two bright attractive girls, Drew.'

'Linda's all right. She's getting keen on that Limey boy and she might do worse. He's got a good job and I like him. Here he is now. You can ask him about the buoy. Hey Martin we need you. Dene here's got a job for you.'

One of the disappointments of Drew's life was that he and his wife Paula hadn't had any sons. Paula had become fairly cool about sex with Drew and for that matter, as they grew up, had become detached about the two girls, Arabella and Belinda — Bella and Linda for short. Paula's mother, a man-sour divorcee had wanted Paula to be a painter and she had only married Drew when it became clear she wouldn't make much of a living as a working artist.

'Living on Limburger in a garret isn't going to suit you, honey,' Drew told her. 'And your Poppa isn't going to will you a fortune. Better marry me and exercise your genius on the ancestral home.'

And so she had. She became an elegant *object d'art* herself, always expensively turned out in impeccable taste. She did over the Campbell house in Baltimore in style, consulting interior decorators, taking trips to Europe and becoming a collector herself. Her collection of *étuis* and snuff-boxes started out with a few items, but had grown steadily in size and rarity. Nowadays she occasionally loaned items for exhibitions and she had become an authority, subscribing to the right magazines and sometimes giving illustrated talks to groups in search of a speaker to fill their winter schedule.

It had meant that the two girls spent a lot of time in the care of hired help. Drew had no objection. Paula's collection was a fine investment and was carefully insured. His marital ardour cooled comfortably. Paula was on hand as a hostess when he needed her, they each had their own friends and he had his stamping ground in the cottage over on Crab Alley. Tucked away from the crowded resorts of St Michaels, Oxford and Cambridge, he had his comfortable power-boat ready to take out week-end parties in the season.

At first both girls had gone to the same local school, but then they had gone their separate ways. Bella was sent to a finishing school and a year at university in Europe from which she returned with a good command of French, a voracious appetite for male attention and a weakness for the latest fashionable fad, whether it was drugs or pop music.

Linda suffered the sharper shocks and more practical disciplines of a nursing course. Lacking Bella's beauty and unused to the admiration and easy acceptance it brought, she developed fewer airs and less of the graceless self will of the modish young. Bella was a centre of attraction, a beauty spoiled and courted. Linda was a plain girl, friendly, practical and with a tough centre.

Martin joined the group, fresh-faced, fit-looking and ready for the race. He waited to hear about the job.

'It's the buoy moored at the outer end of the start for the Hobie Cat race,' Dene explained to him. 'I don't think we've left enough room even allowing for a bit of bunching. Do you think you could arrange to move it farther out?'

'No trouble. I'll get hold of one of the boat boys, Rosco, and go out with him in the launch. I'm not sure if he's got enough chain, though. It falls away and gets deeper suddenly — but I could bend on some nylon rope. It's only for the day. How much farther out should it be?'

'I reckon another thirty yards would do. What do you think Scottie?'

'That should be about right. The trouble with catamarans is they need room.'

'We've just had that fellow Ramón over here,' said Drew to Martin. 'See you beat him good and proper in the race.

It would rile me more than somewhat to see him get that trophy I bought. He gets under my skin worse than a chigger.'

'I've got a good boat and I know the course so if everything goes right . . . well we'll see. How did Bella meet Ramón anyway? Linda hasn't said anything about it.'

'We had a party at the end of the cruise in the Virgins. Linda went back to the boat early. 'You can go and beat up the town,' she said, 'I'm going to hit the hay.' Bella sloped off with Ramón, and me and Dene here — well we got a mite high. What's the harm in that, eh Dene?'

'No harm at all.'

'At least I don't touch dope like the kids nowadays — pot and crack and pills. Stick to clean liquor and good tobacco, that's what I say.' Drew took a half-chewed cigar out of his mouth and looked at it reflectively.

'Well I'd better get on,' said Martin, not wishing to be drawn in; and he left to find the boat boy.

'How about it?' said Drew. 'Time for a highball and a spot of lunch at the bar. That suit you Scottie? No need to ask Dene here.'

'OK. Racing starts at two. You can tell me more about your cruise.'

'Isn't that English couple due up here soon, Drew?' asked Dene. 'They were coming up from Miami by the Intracoastal. Didn't you invite them to visit?'

'The Glazers. Yes, they'll probably stay a piece with us. It could be any time now. They were going to call us when they got to Hampton Roads.'

'They're a couple who sailed across,' Dene explained. 'We met them on our cruise.'

'Sailed across, eh,' said Scottie. 'Quite an achievement. Are they sailing back?'

'Yes — but I think they're looking for a crew this time. He was a dope merchant, wasn't he Drew? Legitimate of course.'

'Yes a chemist in one of the big pharmaceuticals. I think it was Kaufman.'

'Poppa. Hullo, Dene.' It was Linda in

shorts and a T-shirt with an anchor motif and carrying a small duffel bag. 'Poppa, have you seen Martin?'

'Sure, he was here just now. He's gone off to move the marker buoy for the start line. You'll find him in the club launch.'

'Goody. And have you seen Ramón? I have to find him because Bella's disappeared.'

'Disappeared! What do you mean?'

'Oh I don't suppose it's serious. We're going together as crew in the log-canoe race. They are counting on her as a spare helmsman and she hasn't turned up.'

'Ramón was here and said he was going to meet up with her. See if his Rolls is still in the car park.'

'She's been a bit strange lately. As if she'd been drinking — or doping.'

'Tell her she's got to see Doc Williams. I'll speak to Paula. Someone's got to hassle with her and sort her out. It's that damned dago Ramón. We ought to get her away for a trip.'

'A trip? Not the wrong sort of trip . . .'

'No, no, no. A vacation, a cruise or something.'

'Oh, and Poppa, there's been a telephone call. From the Glazers, from Hampton Roads. They'll bring their boat up in a few days.

8

Yacht Race

The light racing cats came dancing round the starting line up to fifteen minutes before the advertised time of the race. They fluttered like moths in a garden, dipping, swerving, standing into the wind with a shiver of sails as they went about, then filling and racing off on the other tack. They had come from far and near, some belonging to Matapeake itself, some sailing down the East Shore or even across the Bay from Susquehanna, Patapsco, Annapolis, Patuxent or the Potomac.

The Clubhouse stood on the south shore of a little bay with the foreshore running nearly east and west. Thus the starting line ran roughly north and south. For the race itself there were three marker buoys: A — one mile to the west of the start; B — one mile south-east of A; and

C — two miles north-north-west of B. The yachts had to pass in succession Buoy A, Buoy B, and Buoy C, taking them all to port. From Buoy C they had to go round A a second time, again leaving it to port and so back to the Clubhouse, crossing the finishing line from west to east. There was a diagram put up on a noticeboard that made it all clear.

The wind was blowing from the south-west so for the first leg boats would be close-hauled. The second leg A to B, would be an easy reach with the wind to starboard. For the third leg, B to C, the boats would have the wind on the port quarter. For the fourth leg C to A they would be close-hauled again having to tack — and for the fifth and final leg back to the Clubhouse they would have an easy run on the starboard tack. All this of course provided the wind stayed steady.

Martin was out early, sailing round and gauging wind and tide. He knew the local conditions and was at home with the boat, having sailed it extensively beforehand. He planned to start from the farthest end of the starting line. Although there was a disadvantage in being to leeward of the other boats, he reckoned to get a better breeze, being less blanketed by the shore, and also having clearer water. Also the tide would help him more since it was starting to run down the shore from north to south. He saw Ramón, lean and rangy, lying across his borrowed boat and controlling it like a toy. In the rest of the field there were some crack competitors from Annapolis, a number of women sailors not to be taken lightly and finally perhaps the largest number of entrants who would take it easy, enjoy the sail and not bust themselves to win.

Martin's tactic at the start paid off handsomely. He crossed the line right on the gun, close-hauled and going fast. He was only a few yards to leeward and had his nose in front of the rest of the fleet. Nearest on his tail was one of the naval cadets, a cheerful all-rounder called Saunders. Ramón was behind but up to windward and still very much in contention. Martin concentrated on getting the best out of the boat, steering carefully through the slight lop got up by the wind against the tide. Even though it was only a fresh breeze he saw out of the tail of his eye that a couple of boats had capsized. They could be righted fairly easily, but it would be enough to put them out of the race.

He saw the buoy looming ahead of him. He had just made it close-hauled on the port tack, without having to go about and without pinching. The boats to windward had to ease their sheets slightly and steer off the wind, so they were now quite clearly a few yards behind. Here was the buoy. He eased the sheet a trifle and bore away, then shot up as he reached the buoy, tacking just beyond it and coming round so as to pass it on the starboard tack. Saunders was right on his heels but was on the port tack and had to give way, while Martin, easing to a reach, was off on the next leg three or four yards clear.

Ramón was in the next bunch with two others and Martin gave him a wave as he surged along on the reach, straining out to windward to keep the weather float down as the wind gusted and blew harder. With the jib let well out he kept the mainsheet in hand, easing it slightly as he felt the wind harden to spill some of the breeze. On this second leg the boats were really flying along balanced on the leeward float and kicking up a shower of spray. As they got to Buoy B they passed out of sight of the watchers in front of the Clubhouse, behind a grove of cottonwoods that lined the shore to the south.

On the shore with the crowd Bella, Linda and Drew were watching and even Paula, elegant in a new outfit, had come down for the occasion.

'Martin!' shouted Linda, binoculars glued to her eyes. 'He's still leading — but only just.'

'Go it! Go it!' bellowed Drew. 'They're great boats.'

'I hope Ray's well up,' said Bella. 'Let me have a look. Poppa, Linda, don't hog the glasses. There, he's nearly third equal. Come on! They're out of sight.'

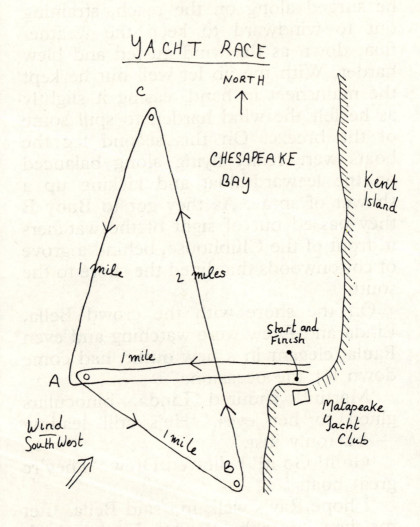

YACHT RACE

NORTH

C

CHESAPEAKE
BAY

Kent
Island

1 mile

2 miles

Start and
Finish

1 mile

A

Wind
South West

1 mile

B

Matapeake
Yacht
Club

'Let me see,' Linda held out her hand. 'Oh — Oh — wait a minute. They're coming into sight. It's — help. It's that Saunders boy. He's leading Martin — only just.'

Saunders, with his advantage in weight balancing the boat had been able to drive his catamaran faster on the reach and had steadily pushed past Martin to windward. Martin tried to luff him but the other kept his advantage and Martin saw that if they got into an all-out luffing match, it would only let the second bunch of boats slip past. Gradually Saunders gained and at the second buoy he was half-a-dozen yards ahead. Here the yachts had to gybe round, with the wind moving across the stern and the boom swinging from port to starboard. Single-handed and with the wind stronger it was a trickier change than the turn into the wind at the previous buoy.

As he went round the buoy Saunders, perhaps elated at going into the lead, let the mainsheet slip out of his hand in a second's inattention. The boom flew over with a bang, brought up hard against the leeward stay. The stay held but the light metal boom made in hollow section was slightly bent. Running before the wind the sail still drew reasonably well and Saunders recovered the sheet and held his lead.

Martin managed to gybe round without accident and on a free run of two miles with the wind astern the pace and motion were both easier. In this race spinnakers were not carried so the competitors were spared the complication of hoisting and setting so temperamental a sail. However it was clearly worth trying to get the jib to draw goose-winged on the side opposite the main. Bearing away a little and pulling the jib round to the windward side, Martin got it to fill and began to gain marginally on Saunders.

Most of the fleet was now round the second buoy and moving before the wind at a more dignified pace. When Martin glanced round he saw that Ramòn had somehow got ahead of the second group and was only a short distance behind him. He moved further aft and fiddled with the sheets. Saunders was evidently worried how his mainsail would draw on the next leg close-hauled with a bent boom. He was trying to correct the bend with his shoulder but in the process he lost the tiller, his boat came up into the wind and both Martin and Ramón passed him. On they went towards the third buoy.

At this buoy they would round up into the wind close-hauled and having to tack to windward. This buoy was the farthest out into the bay, the farthest from the Clubhouse and almost out of sight from the shore. Concentrating hard, Martin rounded the buoy safely then looked round for Ramón, expecting to see him just astern. To his astonishment Ramón was level with him and, what is more, slightly to windward. If he had gone round the buoy it was quite impossible. There was no doubt that he had cheated and gone inside it. Well, thought Martin, sharp practice! The other boats were far enough away and too busy to notice. From the Clubhouse it would be most difficult to pick up. Martin himself could hardly make an official protest since he hadn't actually seen anything.

As if to avoid him Ramón immediately tacked in towards the shore while Martin carried on out into the bay. In Martin's mind the race had become more and more a struggle between himself and Ramón, a struggle that was more than merely a sporting contest — a fight, a punch-up, a duel — something with higher stakes than a yacht race. Another two boats had come up close but they didn't look like overtaking Ramón or him. It seemed as though Martin's tactic of tacking out into the bay was benefiting from the tide and each time they came towards each other Martin proved to be that few yards ahead. He was not sure, however, that it was going to be enough, since on the very last leg when they would be on a broad reach, Bella's boat was a fraction faster.

The next tack brought them to Buoy A, the last leg of the race and Martin was still a couple of yards ahead. Holding himself on his harness out to the limit to windward and flying towards the shore and the finish, Martin prayed that the catamaran would stay upright. He could see the shore coming up fast ahead. The South American was gaining inch by inch. Martin used the same tactic as at the start, aiming for the far end of the line to get the strongest of the wind. Ramón's bow crept past his stern; in another few seconds he would take Martin's wind.

Then Martin was over the line — a gun went — he turned towards the land and rounded up to the landing stages. Ramón brought his boat alongside.

'Oh. So you won. Another minute my friend, and I would have you — *Inglese*.' He put out his hand and closed it in an aggressive gesture.

'Maybe,' Martin answered dryly. 'But you didn't have another minute. Didn't you cut inside that far buoy? I reckon you came up too fast to have gone outside it.'

'O . . . o, so. You are suspicious, my friend. No, no, no. In any case how do you say — all is fair in love and war.'

'But this isn't love — or war.'

'To me life is war. Life is to the strong.'

'Is that so? Don't push too hard. Others can be strong too. Now it's time for a drink.'

★ ★ ★

Did either of them sense that this was not the end of their rivalry and that a deadlier game would eventually be played between them for grimmer stakes?

9

Erotic Variations

The spacious apartment, twelve storeys high above the city, with views to distant cloud-capped hills, was furnished with Arabian Nights luxury. The broad living space was thick with carpet, bright with the glow of Persian rugs and on the walls the fresh colour of carefully-selected paintings. Gardens of exotic plants and flowers were banked on the wide balconies, luxuriant as the hanging gardens of Babylon. In the kitchen there was every conceivable kind of equipment for cooking, freezing and storing. There were chutes for laundry, mail and garbage and at a telephone call a service centre would supply a servant, a luxury meal or a simple snack, books and newspapers, provisions, liquor, mending, massage, manicure. In the bathroom was a vapour shower and the Jacuzzi bath was like a small swimming-pool. The bedroom had heavy skin rugs on the floor and the bed, broad and low as a playing-field, repeated itself in a dazzlement of wall and ceiling mirrors.

* * *

The lovers had been there a night and a day — making love, eating, drinking, drugging, smoking, sleeping, and lounging in the caressing warmth of the sunken bath. The girl was a young beauty, her ripe breasts and firm body bursting, overblown, drunk with a welter of sensation. The man was a dark demon, strong shouldered with slim, muscled torso. In this luxury setting he played the host with an easy flair and a certain lazy sadism, steering the girl sometimes to frustration, sometimes to uncontrollable excess. He would also with an occasional slowly violent gesture, press heavily on the girl's breasts, force a knee into her crutch or give her repeated heavy-handed slaps on the buttocks — rites of subjection and aimed too at erotic arousal.

Now, in the early evening, she was standing naked in the kitchen lacing two cups of coffee with rum. The man came in dressed in a silk robe. Possessively he caressed her firm breasts with his hand.

'Honey, now we can have another joint, eh. Better leave having a trip until later this evening — one of those sweet, sweet dreams.'

'Gee, I'll be high.'

'You'll feel good. It's normal. Enjoy yourself, why not.'

When they had finished their drinks and smokes, he carried her through to the bedroom and began to make love to her again — forcing, dominating, crushing. Under the influence of the drug time lost its meaning, seconds stretched to minutes, minutes to hours. She cried out wildly, incoherently as one possessed in a fit as orgasm followed orgasm and she was shaken by waves of unbearable pleasure.

'How was that, honey?'

'Oh I'll say. I went places I've never been before.'

'Is that so. You haven't been no place

yet. Wait till Karl and Eva come and the four of us get together this evening.'

He started to get dressed and explained to her about Karl and Eva.

'They're my associates and big in the business. As I've told you there's a job for you in the firm and it's time you met them, honey. It's an easy job, no risk to it if you're smart — and big money, everything you want. We've got business to discuss, but we can combine it with a little pleasure, you'll see.'

The words fluttered in her drowsed ears like bright butterflies. Better than being stuck with the family, taking a dull husband, settling down to babies — ugh. Possibly even having to scrape along. But at this stage she still had doubts.

'I'm not sure,' she said. 'Perhaps I ought not to stay this evening.'

'Feel free, honey. No one's going to force you,' but there was a hint of menace in his tone. 'You'd be passing up something special. Of course once you're in, you're in. We don't want anyone spilling trade secrets.'

To interrupt there came the sound of door chimes.

'There they are now, honey. You just have a talk with Eva. You'll love her, she understands women. Now slip into a gown and I'll go and meet them. Don't hurry yourself. We'll start with drinks and I've ordered a super supper.'

★ ★ ★

Eva was early middle-aged, fair-haired, brown, soft-bodied but lithe. Karl in his late forties, had a heavy, sensual face, was medium height and so strong in build that his clothes seemed ready to burst their seams if he squared his shoulders or tensed his muscles. The newcomers came in and hung up their coats as if they were at home.

'Hullo Karl, hullo Eva.'

'Well Ray, how goes it?' They spoke in English as Karl's Spanish was limited, Eva's non-existent.

'I've been socialising more than somewhat, but it's been worth it. I've been able to locate a yacht we could take over for this English operation. How've you and Eva been?'

'We got a marvellous consignment of crack the other day. Had to lean on the supplier a bit, but it was worthwhile. So you've been socialising — you look well on it.'

'You know the girl's here tonight. She's still in the bedroom doing herself up. I've been coping with the family too. Poppa doesn't like me and it's mutual. The mother's busy with her antiques. There's a sister who won't be any help and her boy-friend — *Inglese* and a pain in the arse. But with luck she won't be in touch with any of them when she gets in with us.'

'Good. What about this yacht?'

'It means involving you and Eva to sail it to England. You're ideal to stand in. We'll take it over at sea, the usual business. The girl might be on board. She won't give any trouble. You can see to that.'

'So she's here tonight. How is she?'

'She's all right. You ought to meet your new crew and try her out for future

94

use. She isn't into group sex yet so you and Karl can teach her a thing or two.'

'Will she work with us? No scruples — on the business side?'

'She might need persuading to shut her eyes to some things. But she'll be fine for what we want. Putting up a really good front and handling the stuff discreetly. I might have got her a bit heavy with dope tonight and we might have to regulate things — especially when we're sailing. See what you think. What makes it all easier at present is that she's gone for me in a big way.'

'Sounds as though you've done a good job.'

'Perhaps you'd like to go and see if she's ready, Eva. You know where the main bedroom is. Take her in hand as you know how. Karl and I can discuss details of this English plan.'

Eva nodded and went to find the girl.

'The plans are going ahead well,' said Karl. 'The market's there all right and most of the smuggling is by the usual means. There's some opposition, but we can handle it.'

'We've got good people for that.'

'You can go over from New York, Ray. The diesel yacht is ready to go straight away. Take the boys. Once we're established in London we could go on and base the boat in France where I've got a few connections.

★ ★ ★

Eva knocked on the bedroom door and went in.

'Hullo dear, I'm Eva. That dress looks lovely. My, what a terrific figure you've got. Mmm — those hips. We've been hearing about you. How clever you are and how you might be able to work with us. It's a wonderful job — travelling, adventure, variety. Ray's a real man, isn't he? So is my friend Karl. You'll like him. And he'll like you at once — mmm, he couldn't help it. Now, when you're ready, we're going to have a few drinks and a grand dinner. And then we can really enjoy ourselves.'

10

Letter Home

My dear Annette,

Since I last wrote from the West Indies we've covered quite a lot of water. We've sailed or motored up the Intra-Coastal Waterway — they call it 'the Ditch' — over 900 miles from Miami right up to Hampton Roads on the south side of Chesapeake Bay. At St Thomas in the Virgins we met some nice Americans, a sailing family — father and friend and two daughters. They are right into boats except for the wife who's artistic, and they invited us to stay with them in Baltimore. Mr Campbell — Drew (American isn't it) — lent us his motor-boat and we explored the nooks and crannies of the Bay area. Linda, the younger girl, showed us round and it seems we just missed a most exciting Regatta at the local yacht club. Her English boy-friend (comes from

Hampshire but he's over here for a while seconded by his London insurance firm) won a catamaran race and the two girls came third crewing in a race for bigger boats — 'log-canoes' they're called. We had lunch at the Club and very smart it was. She took us to some lovely lonely spots down near the mouth of the bay. We also spent a day in Washington and saw the sights and we were able to get to the famous Naval College in Annapolis and see it as far as it's open to visitors.

The last week-end we stayed at their home in Baltimore and they threw a big party. There Paula, the artistic wife, showed us her wonderful collection of enamels. She's been collecting them for years and they must be worth a fortune. They were *étuis* and snuff-boxes mostly, but there was a super French spectacle-case and an Italian mirror-back showing a Court of Love!

It turned out there was some method in their kindness, at least as Drew confessed to us, since we were looking for somebody to crew on the voyage back to England, they would like it if we took their older daughter, Bella. It seems father wants to get her away from an overzealous boy-friend, though I must say he seemed rich and charming-mannered enough — South American. It's the old story, daughter's headstrong, father doesn't approve, so it's a cruise to England to get her away from him. When we asked her she agreed, so it's all fixed for her to come with us. We can find her accommodation in England or she could stay on board for a while. We're not going to bust ourselves getting back. We're going to stop at Bermuda and we might stop at the Azores — so don't expect us in a hurry.

It'll be nice having an extra hand and I only hope she doesn't mope too much for her South American. There are still a few things to do before we sail and we've got guests for lunch so I'd better stop. Eric sends his best wishes. Love and good wishes and see you soon.

Yours ever, Greta.

11

Farewell Party

Since Bella seemed to be away from home a lot seeing friends and saying goodbye, it was Linda who looked after the Glazers on two of her days off from the hospital. On one occasion they were able to visit one of the uninhabited islands off the east shore of the Peninsula, where the Virginia Nature Conservancy preserves the natural eco-system and provides breeding grounds for some animals, water-fowl, fish and plant life. On the second outing they drove to Annapolis and Washington and spent a day sightseeing — the Smithsonian complex, the Wax Museum, the Corcoran Gallery, the Shakespeare Library, the White House, the Capitol, the Lincoln Museum . . .

'Who said America had no history?' Greta remarked. 'There's as much to see here as in a European city. It's great but I'm worn out. It makes sailing seem a lazy pastime.'

Now it was the weekend of departure. Bella had surfaced and got her things on board *Milady*. The Glazers were staying a couple of nights in the Campbell's Baltimore house and Paula and Drew were throwing a farewell party for Bella and the visitors on the final Sunday evening. There was dancing and supper with about sixty guests, a mixture of young and middle-aged. As it was a warm summer evening the party spilled over into the garden and went on until after midnight. Ramón was conspicuous by his absence since he had had to go on to New York on business. He had just had time to meet the Glazers before he left. Bella, surrounded by a squadron of young beaux including some boys from Annapolis, seemed not too upset at having parted from her Latin lover. Drew congratulated himself on his generalship.

'You see, you've got to have finesse,' he told his friend Dene. 'At least she won't be disappearing for nights on end.

If she isn't here we'll know where she is. And by the time three months is up and she's back here, he'll have forgotten her even if she hasn't forgotten him.'

'Sure. Do you know how we made out on the Regatta?' said Dene. 'We made a profit. A profit — after all we spent. It just shows you.'

'Is that so?' said Drew absently, more interested in his own train of thought. 'You see the Latin isn't the sticking type — not like young Martin.'

In the house Greta and Eric were talking to Paula.

'We've had a wonderful time,' said Greta. 'I do hope you can come some time and stay with us in Hampshire — Hampshire England, that is.'

'I'd like to. But Drew doesn't like Europe much. Too much art for him.'

'Perhaps Linda will come. She's been so good taking us round.'

'She's wedded to her nursing. But she might.'

'You could come with her and pick up something for your collection,' Eric suggested.

'On my own without Drew I only go over if I hear from a dealer. Half-a-dozen know me and the word gets around. Or if there's a big sale. It's not much good going over on spec. These enamels don't grow in the garden.'

'No indeed. What about security bringing them back? Aren't you afraid of being robbed?' said Greta, fingering a piece. 'They're so small.'

'When I'm travelling the airline or the hotel look after them. And in between I'm afraid I sometimes pop them into my handbag. As you say a snuff-box can be as small as a cigarette lighter. That way Customs don't usually bother me. Here as you can see they're all in cabinets fronted with wired glass. The keys are hidden in a drawer and the house itself has a burglar alarm. The insurance sent a man and he was satisfied. It's the firm Martin's seconded to, but of course he's in the marine insurance branch.'

'Then we couldn't go out for a walk in the garden in the small hours unless we wanted to wake the dead.'

'That's right.'

'Paula dear, we must go,' a guest interrupted, 'it's been a lovely party.'

'Mrs Glazer, I hope you have a fine passage across to England.'

'Paula darling, it's been good to see you.'

'Thank you for a lovely party.'

'Don't forget sailing next week-end.'

'Thursday for lunch. I'll call to fix everything.'

'Thanks again, we had a lovely time.'

Gradually the guests drifted away, car lights came on, engines revved up, tyres crackled over the gravel drive. The family party and house guests were left alone.

'Perhaps we ought to go back and sleep on board,' said Eric Glazer.

'Have a comfortable night ashore,' said Drew warmly. 'Your room's all ready — the one you had last night. You're not sailing until afternoon.'

'Linda will take you down after breakfast,' said Paula.

'Sure I will. I don't have to be at the hospital until eleven.'

'Well that's good of you,' Greta agreed. 'We have got everything ready thanks to

Linda's help. There's only some fresh food to buy. I want to write a short note to a friend. And Paula, come down with Bella and have lunch on board. You haven't been on the boat and we'll be lying alongside until we go, so you just have to step on board. That town marina's very handy.'

'All set fair for a fine crossing then,' Drew concluded. Bermuda — Azores — Plymouth. I wish I was coming along.'

'So long as we don't meet a hurricane,' said Eric. We've been lucky so far. The worst dusting we got was crossing the Bay going down to Vigo.'

'Oh you'll soon be out of the range of hurricanes. It's a mite early in the season too — late July, it's hardly August. How long do you reckon it'll take?'

'If we do a hundred miles a day that's fair for us. Say thirty-five days across with ports. We ought to be there by September.'

'Let's have a last one to celebrate,' said Drew, helping himself. But no one else seemed interested.

'It seems a long time to me,' said

Paula. 'Well I'm for bed. See you all at breakfast.'

'Good night.'

'Good night.'

'Oh Dinah, there you are. See everything's locked up after the party caterer's have finished, please. Don't forget to put the alarm on.'

'Sure ma'am.'

★ ★ ★

About three o'clock the next day after lunch on board, Eric started the engine of the little boat. Greta and Bella at bow and stern slipped the mooring ropes and Greta pushed the bow out. Going slow ahead *Milady* curved out and moved down among the fishing boats and the big container ships, away from her quiet corner of the waterfront. Men on a cargo boat stopped working to see them go. A skipper on a menhaden fishing-boat waved to them.

'Bye, Mom,' called Bella.

Paula waved her hand as she watched them head down the Patapasco out to

Chesapeake Bay. Then, after a minute or two, she turned and walked back to her car.

Would she have waved longer, if she had known she would never see Bella again?

12

Burglary

The house seemed empty after Bella and the Glazers had gone, so on Tuesday Paula called an old art school friend who had a pottery business in the country near Brunswick and drove over to visit her. She stayed overnight and came back on Wednesday since on Thursday she had to meet a photographer who was taking pictures of one of her pieces to illustrate a new Italian art history — a fifteenth-century Florentine pyx in painted enamel.

The two cabinets that housed the collection were in a room on the second floor that had originally been a nursery, and which doubled as Paula's study and studio. There was one key for the two locks kept in a bottom drawer of her desk. Each cabinet held some fifty items on velvet-covered shelves. *In situ* it was difficult to see them properly, and to show them Paula had a small covered table where they could be seen, admired and handled, and the fine work looked at through a glass. A tiny number was pasted under each piece and a corresponding card in an index carried a history, a description and a photo.

On Thursday Drew had left for his office and Linda was on duty over at the hospital, so Paula was alone in the house with the maid. At half-past-nine she went up to the studio — then ten minutes later there came a piercing shriek from the studio and Paula rushed out on to the landing.

'Dinah! Dinah!' she shouted down the stairs. 'It's a robbery. My enamels.'

'Call master. Call the police,' Dinah advised her, hurrying from below.

Paula's trembling fingers misdialled twice before she got connected.

'Drew, Drew,' her voice was shrill when he came on the line. 'Can you come over — now. We've been robbed!'

'What!'

'The enamels. I went to get the pyx

this morning. You know that man from Harcourt Brace was coming — is coming. The pyx is here, but other things are missing.'

'What? What's gone?'

'I haven't checked properly yet — can you come over?'

'Sure. But I can't right now. I couldn't do much anyway. You'd better phone the police — no, I'll call them. I know one of the lieutenants in our precinct. What's his name — Hudson. I'll be over as soon as I can. Maybe you shouldn't touch anything.'

Near lunch time Drew arrived with the lieutenant and another officer. Paula was still shaken by the loss, but she had managed to check what was missing and cope with the photographer, who, to leave the field clear in the study had got the pyx downstairs and set up his lights in the dining-room, supervised by Dinah.

Hudson looked carefully at the cabinets, while the man with him took some photos and tested for prints. Then he looked round the room, checked the windows, looked at the room from outside, checked the burglar alarm, came up again and got out his notebook.

'First, how were they locked up?'

'Just by a key. I kept it in a drawer of that desk. But there's a burglar alarm for the house.'

'Hmm. The thieves could've opened the locks with picks — if they were professionals. Again they might have found the key in the desk. Or it might have been someone who knew where you kept the key.'

'The key was hidden in the drawer, but someone might have noticed where I put it. *You* knew, Drew, where it was, and I suppose the girls knew.'

'Was the burglar alarm on all the time?'

'It was always put on at night. We had a party on Sunday that went on late so it wasn't on until the guests and caterers left.'

'Would it stop anyone already in the house coming into this room?'

'No, it wouldn't. I'd lock this door if I went away but not if I was sleeping in the house.'

'Now can you tell me in detail what's missing?'

'There are five pieces. A Limoges plaque in grisaille depicting Saint Christopher, size 8 by 10 centimetres; two English pocket snuff-boxes in painted enamel, one with a green-leaf design, the other showing a hunting scene, both about 6 centimetres long; a Japanese lineless enamel cameo of a woman with a fan by Sosuke, 4 centimetres in diameter; and a champlevé enamel bowl from Ireland, 7 centimetres in diameter. That one was *twelfth-century*. I've got photos and drawings of them all.'

'What were they worth?'

'A hell of a lot,' said Drew. 'They were some of our best.'

'That's true,' Paula agreed. Some of the bigger things were more valuable, like the pyx. The things stolen are all small items that could be tucked away in a small space.'

'What *were* they worth?'

'I've got here what I paid. The Irish bowl was the most expensive — 8000 dollars. Then 400, 1400, 300 (that was a bargain, brought back by a GI I think) and 750. That makes nearly 11000 spent over the last ten to fifteen years. They could be worth five times that today — say 55000.'

'Jeez, just those five items? That makes over a million for the whole collection.'

'Something like that — if we had a good sale.'

'I don't get it,' said Lieutenant Hudson. 'No fence is going to touch this lot. Unless it's a commissioned job for a crank collector — rolling in dough and a crook into the bargain. Or else it's an amateur job. There's no sign of a break-in. When did you last see the things that are missing?'

I'm sure it was all there last Friday. I dusted the pyx that was to be photographed and got it ready. Then for luck I went over the other shelves and the other cabinet with a duster. There was nothing missing then, I'm sure. I've shown the collection since, but I'm always careful to check that each piece I take out for viewing goes back, that everything's there and that I lock up afterwards.'

'Who knew about the collection?'

'Family, Baltimore friends. Any collectors in the same line.'

'Did any visitors see it after last Friday?'

'There was an English couple visiting. My daughter Bella's sailing with them to England. They did stay in the house a couple of nights.'

'So they had the knowledge and the opportunity?'

'Oh I don't think it was them. They seemed very respectable and honest.'

'You never know,' said Drew frowning.

'There was also Bella's friend, Ramón. I showed him the collection about a week ago,' said Paula.

'He's the one!' Drew exclaimed. 'It's that dago for sure. He's smart and light-fingered.'

'My husband's prejudiced, lieutenant. Ramón was attracted by my elder daughter. That's why we arranged for her to go off on this cruise to England.'

'Was it a case of the poor young fortune hunter?'

'No sir, he was loaded. A rich South American. And he wasn't all that young.'

'I could check on him. Where is he now? Have you got his address?'

'I expect Bella's got his address. All we know is that he went to New York on business before we had the party.'

'Did he stay in the house at all?'

'No. Only down at the cottage one week-end. He was here on the Saturday to say goodbye.'

'Uh huh. You both live here. Who else?'

'My daughter, Bella, before she left on this voyage. But she was away a lot staying with friends. Then there's my other daughter, Linda. She does nursing over at Essex Hospital and has an apartment near. But she was staying here on vacation recently and she often stays overnight when she has a day off.'

'How about servants?'

'We've only got one maid, Dinah. She's been here years. For the party we had Krafts the caterers. They sent three people.'

'I'll check that out. I'll talk to them.'

'Thank you, lieutenant.'

'That's about it then. Maybe I can talk to the maid now. I'll see your nursing daughter later. Could you call her at the hospital and ask her to drop in at the station when she's off duty? The three on the yacht are out of it for the moment. But it might be worthwhile writing to them about the robbery and getting their reactions.'

'Right. We'll do that, lieutenant.'

'I'll have the descriptions circulated. But if it has any result I'll be surprised. You can't expect it. I suppose it was all insured?'

'Sure, Golden Eagle. I called them from the office. They're sending a man tomorrow.'

'I'd like to talk to him when he's looked round. It's likely he gets to handle more of these cases than I do.'

'Thanks very much, lieutenant.'

'That's OK, Ma'am — Mr Campbell — I hope you get your stuff back.'

13

Disappearance

When Linda called from the hospital and told Paula she was going to see the lieutenant at the station that afternoon, Paula suggested that after she had seen the police, she should come on afterwards for dinner.

'Oh dear, I had a date with Martin. But maybe I could bring him with me. OK?'

When they got to the house around seven, Linda was sympathetic about the robbery, but there was something else on her mind.

'I couldn't tell that policeman a thing,' she said. 'Oh Mom, I'm sorry.'

'It was a shock. It's the first time I've ever been burgled.'

'I'll fix the bastards when we get them,' said Drew. 'That stuff was worth a mint.'

'Dad, Mom, I wanted Martin to come over tonight — we wanted to tell you. You see Martin and I want to get engaged. I hope it's OK with you two?'

'Oh darling, that's marvellous!'

'What about you, Poppa? OK?'

'Sure it's OK. With Annapolis just over the way, I thought one of you girls might marry into the Navy. That Saunders is a smart lad. I know his family too. I guess it'll have to be Bella.'

'Oh Poppa. He's too brash for Bella. In any case you'll meet Martin's family.'

'If it's any help, Mr Campbell, my father wasn't Navy, but he was in the Army. He's retired now but he was a Major. Not a bad regiment either. They fought at Waterloo.'

'Well I can't argue against that. We'd better open some champagne and drink a toast.'

'There's another thing might influence you,' said Martin. 'In my experience Army people are keener on yacht racing and they win more races — more than Navy people.'

118

'Well you did beat that Saunders boy. And more important you beat that damn dago, Ramón. Well done.'

'We've talked about what we're going to do,' said Linda. Obviously Martin's job's more important than my nursing and he has got to go back to England when his secondment's over. But there is a chance he might get a permanent job with the firm over here.'

'You'll just have to play it as it works out,' said Drew. 'There's a lot to think about.'

'The wedding — that's the thing,' said Paula. 'Oh a big wedding will be lovely. And Martin, your father and mother could come over.'

'Dad would enjoy a trip over here,' said Martin. 'He'd love to see the sailing scene. But Linda says she doesn't want a big wedding.'

'You don't mind, Mom, do you? Keep the big wedding for Bella. I've got my nursing to concentrate on — I will go on nursing either here or in England.'

'I could see to the arrangements.

But there, if you don't want a big wedding . . . You must do what you want.'

'Well, here's to the happy couple.' Drew, who had served them all with a celebratory drink, raised his glass.

About ten days after this conversation, Paula and Drew got postcards from Bella saying that they had arrived in Bermuda and Linda got a letter:

Dear Poppa,
    We had rather a slow passage to Bermuda but comfortable enough. Only two days over Force 5 and more often around 2 or 3. Sou'westers to start, then tacking against head winds the last day. Greta and I share the cooking. Eric does the middle watch. I've written Mom. Bella.

Dear Mom,
    We got to Bermuda yesterday and I got your letter about the burglary. I guess the insurance will pay and you'll be able to get better things to fill

the cases. I haven't got Ray's address except a bank in Caracas. He's writing me post restante in Plymouth when we arrive. Love, Bella.

Dearest Linda,

We're having a couple of days ashore here in a hotel which is really luxurious after the yacht. It wasn't a bad passage but duller than our Caribbean cruise — such a slow boat. The Glazers are OK — except he clicks his falsetto when he's eating and she puts 'my dear' into almost everything she says. I miss Ray a lot, life went into high gear when he was around. I'll see him again whatever Poppa says, maybe in England since his business is international. No slow poke, hearty Anglo-Saxons for me. I know you and Martin will get married and make the ideal couple but that's different. Now it's time to go. See you some day. Bella.

At the same time Paula received a thank-you note from the Glazers:

Dear Paula,

Our most cordial thanks for your wonderful hospitality. We've had such a wonderful holiday we can't think of settling again in dull old England, and our stay in your area was the real highlight. Bella's been great as a help with the sailing and cooking, I hope it hasn't been dull for her. You must come over and visit us before long. I *am* sorry about your stolen things and I hope you recover them. I suppose they could be quite valuable. All good wishes to Drew, Linda and yourself. Eric and Greta.

The days went by after these letters had arrived without any further news being received or expected. The yacht had no transmitter on board and though they had made an arrangement for passing on any messages from regular shipping that might sight the yacht, any sightings were unlikely, as between Bermuda and the Azores, *Milady* would not be near any regular shipping lanes.

Nothing was found out about the

robbery. Drew rang Lieutenant Hudson once or twice at intervals, but the lieutenant admitted he was 'fresh outa clues and outa ideas.' A month after the robbery Drew mentioned the matter to the Police Commissioner when he was introduced to him at a Rotary Club luncheon and the latter promised to look into it personally. However, he rang a couple of days later. Though he had put another man on the case to try and find 'some fresh angle' he didn't think they were likely to make a breakthrough. It wasn't in line with any local criminal's work. It didn't tie up with anything they had on their files. Reports of the loss had been circulated everywhere but without result. There was nothing for it but to close the case.

Gradually the days ran into weeks and the weeks ran on.

'Drew, it's nearly four weeks since we had those cards from Bermuda,' said Paula one morning. 'They reckoned to get to the Azores in three weeks at the outside. They're overdue, Drew. We ought to do something.'

Drew set in hand enquiries for the yacht *Milady* through the Coastguard Service. Replies came filtering back. There was no report of the yacht having called at Angra do Heroismo, the intended port of call in the Azores. It was possible she had called at another port, Horta or Ponta Delgada or at one of the smaller islands or put into a sheltered bay where there would be no record — but it didn't seem likely.

Drew persisted with his enquiries and extended them to England. He telephoned the number the Glazers had given but he could get no reply — it appeared the telephone had been cut off. Their home was near Brockenhurst in Hampshire and the house had been let during their absence. An urgent letter addressed to Mr and Mrs E. Glazer/occupier/or agent, Rose Cottage, Picket Lane, Brockenhurst, brought a reply from the House Agent who wrote that the period of the lease having expired, and the tenants having vacated, the house was empty awaiting the Glazer's return.

Then out of the blue came a piece of news that was both reassuring and alarming. In reply to a letter which Drew had written on spec to the Harbour Master's office at Plymouth, England, there came an official confirmation that a private yacht, *Milady* had cleared Customs returning from a cruise to the West Indies and the United States. On board was the owner E. Glazer and two crew. The date was 5 September, the last port of call Bermuda and the intended destination Lymington. But when they cabled Lymington there was no record of the yacht having arrived.

Going by the letters they had received, the yacht would have left Bermuda on 7 August. To get to Plymouth by 5 September it looked as though they had gone direct without calling at the Azores. Why pass up such an attractive port of call? Why, now it was mid-September, was there no mail? Why especially hadn't Bella written? Why hadn't the Glazers gone back to their house at Brockenhurst? Why were there no reports of the yacht? Why? Why?

The day after this news came, Paula and Drew got Linda and Martin to come over in the evening and the four of them held a council of war.

'Something serious has happened. I'm worried about Bella,' said Paula.

'I agree, Mom. There's something wrong. Don't you think so Martin — — Poppa?'

'Yeah, but what? Tell me what . . . ' Drew appealed to them all.

'Could the yacht have been run down at night? In the English Channel?' Linda asked. 'Isn't it lousy with shipping? Suppose they were sunk without being reported — or even without the other ship realising it. Martin?'

'It's a possibility. But the traffic is worse up near the Straits of Dover. Then going from Plymouth to the Isle of Wight (that's where Lymington is) they'd keep near the land and even if they tacked out they'd hardly get into the shipping lane.'

'I'll tell you what's happened,' said Drew excitedly. 'It's the Glazers. They had the chance when they were staying here. They're the ones who got into those cabinets and lifted Paula's enamels.'

'How?' asked Paula.

'Easy. They just watched carefully where you got the key and where you put it away. Then they crept in that last night when they were staying and hid the stuff in their luggage.'

'They were staying actually in the room next door to where the collection is,' Paula admitted. 'It's in the old nursery.'

'But what's that got to do with Bella not writing?'

'Bella might have found the stuff on the yacht — and they had to keep her mouth shut.'

'No . . . ' Paula exclaimed in alarm at the idea.

'You've got to face it. Something's happened. Maybe they kidnapped her and they're holding her until they can unload the stolen goods — or worse.'

'Bella was in some strange moods before she left,' said Linda.

'Yeah, that dago. But he's out of it now. Glazer now was in pharmaceuticals — drugs! Maybe it was a different kind of drugs — dope. The Commissioner was talking about it. It isn't uncommon for people who handle legitimate drugs to get mixed up with the illegal stuff — doctors too. The Commissioner ought to know.'

'But they were such normal people.'

'That could have been a blind. I reckon I'll write to his company. Didn't he mention Kaufman, the pure drugs people?'

'Did the police ever check on Ramón?' Martin asked.

'Bella didn't give us his address,' Linda replied. 'A name's not much to go on.'

'I'm reporting her missing,' Drew announced. 'Official. The Commissioner says they've got a good set-up over there for missing persons. You have to give details and a photo and it can go through Interpol. They might send it to more than one country. I'll put 'abduction suspected'.'

'Add 'or accident'. That'll make it wider,' Martin suggested.

'Can we do anything else?' asked Linda.

'I've got a suggestion,' said Martin seriously. 'Linda and I have put off getting married hoping Bella could come back and my parents would come over . . . '

'That's right, darling. I wanted to have Bella there.'

'My secondment's still got a month to go — but we could get married with just you two and a few of Linda's friends coming. I think I could get my secondment shortened and take the leave I'm due. Then if Linda can get off her nursing we could go over and see if we can find out what's happened.'

'That's a marvellous idea,' said Linda. 'We could make a honeymoon of it and if we found Bella that would round it off.'

'It's more likely to get results then just reporting to the police and writing letters,' said Martin.

'It's not a bad idea,' said Drew. 'I reckon Martin's the persistent sort and you get results more if you're there in person. I can't get away from business just now or I'd go myself. What do you say Paula?'

'I'm afraid I don't want to go just

now. I say let Linda and Martin go. I can make the arrangements for a small wedding, that's no trouble.'

'Would it be any help if I talked to your bosses at Golden Eagle?' said Drew. 'I know one of them as a result of this burglary.'

'I'll see how I get on. If I need heavy ammunition I'll let you know.'

'Then that's all settled. Here's Dinah to tell us dinner's ready. Let's go and eat.'

14

First Enquiries

Let's go over our plans again,' said Martin.

They were on a plane flying in to Heathrow. It was after dark and the suburbs of London lay beneath them like a dark cloak decorated with lines and clusters of brilliant embroidery. A softer black band indicated where the reaches of the Thames spread across the fabric of the night.

'It's lovely,' said Linda to herself, 'like a beautiful woman dressed up for a party. Bella's seen all this. It's new to me. I wonder where she is — that is if she's still . . . '

'Let's go over what we're going to do,' Martin repeated.

'I was spellbound, sorry. Isn't it great!'

'Yes, it's noisy for Londoners but it shows the place off.'

'You can't fly over New York like this. You might catch your bottom on a skyscraper. You said let's go over what we're going to do?'

'I did. I'll have to report to my Insurance Company and ring up the family. Then I'll be free to concentrate on the search. We're booked a couple of nights in the Regent Palace, then if we still want to stay in London we can stay at my Club. I was able to join the Naval Club because of my yachting. I should have mentioned the Club to your Pa.'

'What about seeing your family?'

'If we haven't time to go down to them straight away, I'm sure they'll come up to London for the day to meet you. They often come up for a show or for shopping. We can all stay down in Lyndhurst when we've found Bella.'

'Oh I hope we find her soon.'

'We've got to do some detective work and I'm afraid we're the detectives — criminal investigators perhaps.'

'We're a fine pair of detectives. I'm trained to take pulses not fingerprints.'

'I'm hardly an expert either. But I expect it's persistence and common sense. Elementary my dear Watson.'

'Or the little grey cells, as that Belgian said. I suppose we can imitate the experts.'

'I've got a soft spot for Columbo — modesty in a raincoat. Better than the snobbish Wimsey or Nero Wolfe, bad-tempered overweight and immobile, or Ellery Queen, too clever by half.'

'If it's American I'd rather go for those dramatic Perry Mason court scenes. But if it's British television, we've got the morose Inspector Frost — or Inspector Morse for a bit of culture.'

'Well from Sherlock Holmes onward we've got plenty of fictional models. They work the whole thing out from clues. Have we got enough clues — or the right brains to work them out?'

'At least we're well read in the literature and we've got a theoretical grounding. But it won't cut much ice in a practical world. I expect in a practical world we'll have to rely on the experts behind desks with their files, their computers and their contacts and the people on the ground making enquiries. *We* just have to decide who we have to see and what questions to ask.'

'I suggest,' said Linda seriously, 'Scotland Yard first, Bureau of Missing Persons. Then — '

'Then Customs, Plymouth — the man who went on board *Milady* if we can find him. Then maybe the Coastguard Service. They might now be able to tell us if *Milady* was sighted or if anything came ashore and was reported.'

'Don't forget Mom's stuff and her contacts. Van Loon and Bonnet are the dealers she thinks most of. They might put us in touch with others and we could spread the word we're looking for good enamel work. It might lead to the stolen things.'

'That's a long shot. We're a few thousand miles from where the goods were stolen,' said Martin. 'But you never know.'

★ ★ ★

Their discussion was interrupted and resumed, interrupted and resumed — while the aircraft touched down and taxied to the docking bay, while the passengers walked to the baggage collection, while they passed through Customs and Immigration and while they caught a bus to the town terminal.

'Now for a cab to the hotel,' Linda proposed.

'Tut tut. You mean a taxi,' Martin reproved her. 'Here you eat biscuits not crackers, you burn paraffin not kerosene, you go by Tube not the Subway . . . '

'Yes, my English isn't that bad, darling,' said Linda. 'You put petrol not gas in your car not your auto, you go to the pictures not the movies, you throw away rubbish not garbage, you wear a dressing-gown not a bathrobe . . . '

'Very good. I expect, as you're in Blighty not the Bowery, you'd say bottom for butt, belch for burp and underdone for rare, and watch the leaves fall in the autumn rather than drop in the fall.'

'We get it all here man,' said the taxi driver, 'from Cockney to Czech,

Japanese to Jamaican — that's where I come from.'

They got to the hotel off Piccadilly and Martin went in first with a couple of cases. But when he came back to the taxi for the rest of the luggage Linda was not there.

'The lady saw someone and ran down the road and into the Tube,' said the cabby. 'She called out — tell my husband — I'm going to follow her.'

Martin paid off the taxi and stood there wondering what to do. Finally he took the remaining bags into the hotel and left them at the reception desk. Then he came out again and walked slowly in the direction the driver had pointed.

'Now Linda's disappeared — everyone's disappearing,' he said to himself. 'It's like a science-fiction film.' But as he got to the entrance of the Tube, Linda came toiling up the steps looking dishevelled and upset.

'Oh Martin, Martin.' Ignoring the heedless, hurrying crowd she threw herself into his arms and burst into tears. 'I thought I saw Bella and an older woman who could have been Greta Glazer. I ran after them into the subway, but they had passes for the barrier and I lost them. Oh I lost them. I bought a ticket and tried to follow them but it was hopeless — they'd gone. It's a maze down there — different lines, different directions.'

'Honey, cheer up, honey. It doesn't matter. At least if it was Bella she's alive and free. We'll find her. Now let's go and shake down in our room — it's on a quiet street the receptionist said — have a bath and explore the double bed. Then let's go out and have the best meal London can offer. How's that for a programme?'

Linda looked more cheerful and hugged his arm. 'Sounds OK to me. You're a darling.'

15

More Enquiries

The next day Martin phoned his family. They already knew about Bella's disappearance and agreed it made sense for Martin and Linda to stay in town and concentrate on the search, even though they were on their honeymoon.

'Especially as you think you saw her in a London street,' his mother said. 'We'll come up and see you and meet Linda this week in town. We've got seats for a revival of Shaw on Wednesday so we'll come up in the morning and meet you for lunch at the Club. See if you can get seats too and come to the show — it's *Saint Joan*. That is if Linda isn't too upset about her sister. And if the play isn't too way out, as I know you're a stickler for the original staging. I believe in this version Saint Joan keeps smoking cigarettes to steady her nerves during interrogation. It's been modernised you see — or perhaps it misses being right up to date now we've all given up smoking. You must please yourselves, but we'll have lunch anyway — we're so looking forward to meeting Linda.'

Linda herself phoned the antique dealers. The mention of Paula's name produced the promise of an interview with Pieter van Loon, a director of van Loon and Bonnet. It would have to be the following week as he was away on business.

Martin went in the same day to see his insurance people and promised to report for work when his leave was finished. He also phoned Scotland Yard and the harbour branch of the Customs office in Plymouth. Next week was the earliest he could get an appointment with anyone at the Yard who dealt with missing persons. However, he was able to fix a meeting with a Customs officer in Plymouth at the end of the week, on the Saturday following their arrival.

They took an overnight train to

Plymouth on Friday, leaving Paddington late in the evening.

'What dinky little beds,' exclaimed Linda when they went into the sleeper. 'It's like being in a yacht. Gosh I can't get away from the subject.'

'I shouldn't tell you this perhaps, but they had a fatal fire on this train once,' Martin informed her. 'The report I read at the time said it was people in a sleeper from Plymouth to London. We'd better not lock the door, though there's not the same danger as we don't smoke.'

'Oh how horrible. The burns cases I've had to deal with have been the worst of the lot. Could it — could it have happened to *Milady*?'

'Hardly possible, I'd say. Too many boats around and coastguards on shore. If she went on fire she'd be visible for miles. Anyhow they could always get off in the dinghy. Unless there was an explosion — '

'You mean the bottled gas they use for cooking?'

'Yes — or petrol for the outboard engine. Diesel for the main engine would be safe enough. But an explosion would be spotted the same as a fire.'

★ ★ ★

Early in the morning they stopped in Plymouth in a shunted-off coach and were awakened at seven. Then after washing and dressing, and breakfasting on bacon and eggs in the station café, they walked into town. Their appointment at the Customs office, Millbay Docks was not until 10.30.

It had started off a wet, grey autumn day, the death of summer heavy in the air. The leaves, beginning to fall, were chased by a sullen wind through the littered streets into choked gutters. Then as they walked hand in hand clouds cleared from the sky and a gentle sun turned the ragged trees from dirty yellow to soft gold. They had time to climb up to the Hoe and look all around on to the wide waters of the harbour. There was a warship at anchor out near the breakwater at the entrance and already yachts were moving about, travelling to a

141

rendezvous for Saturday racing or starting a weekend cruise.

'That's what we ought to be doing,' said Linda ' — messing about in boats, not in detective work.'

'Let's hope the detective work eventually leads us to a boat — not to mention a yachtswoman.'

'*Milady* could be holed up anywhere. Even this harbour stretches for miles and there must be dozens of other harbours.'

'Afraid you're right,' Martin nodded gloomily.

'And Bella might be a prisoner on board . . . ' Now Linda's imagination was taking over.

'Anything's possible. But there are so many boats about in most places, they could hardly keep her a prisoner in the cabin . . . Unless she was tied up. Anyone can be immobilised by tape nowadays.'

'Ugh, horrors. If the Glazers were in a drug racket they might have persuaded Bella to go in with them. She was certainly into drugs in some way and she didn't confide in me.'

'We've got to find out. Let's go and talk to the people who saw the yacht. It's nearly time for our appointment. Millbay is over that way.' When they found their way into the docks and located the Customs office, they were shown into an upstairs room with windows overlooking one of the docks. The sound of winches handling cargo came faintly through.

'You're the people asking about an American girl?' said the man behind the littered desk.

'Yes, Bella Campbell. I'm her sister Linda, and this is my husband, Martin Firth. We're over from Baltimore — on holiday — ' Linda blushed, not wanting to admit to being on her honeymoon. 'But our main concern is to find out about my sister — and the boat.'

'We'll do what we can of course. I suppose you want to see the entry for the yacht and talk to the inspector who went on board? The case of your sister, Mrs Firth, is really one for the police.'

'We're going to Scotland Yard next week,' said Martin, not wanting Linda to do all the talking.

'The boat is more our business,' said the senior Customs man. 'It has been reported missing. Any missing or stolen boat is reported to all the police and coastguard stations and to our other Customs offices. We'll do what we can, but first if you want to see all the documents, have you brought any identification?'

'Yes, of course,' said Martin. 'Will our credit cards do? And here's the letter we got from you saying the yacht had arrived in Plymouth.'

'That's fine,' said the official, reading. 'The yacht *Milady* reported and cleared Customs and Immigration etc etc. Well the man you want, Inspector Primmer, is out with a yacht at the moment but he won't be long. If you'd like to wait he'll come and talk to you here. I've got some business downstairs so if you'll excuse me.' He got up and left them anxiously sitting on the edge of their seats waiting for what they hoped would give a clue to what had happened.

In another five minutes Inspector Primmer came in and introduced himself.

He was in uniform, not a brass button out of place, meticulous from his well-brushed hair to the shining toes of his shoes. His appearance gave assurance that within a narrow, well-defined range, everything would be professionally precise and well-ordered.

'Now sir — madam. Here are copies of the crew list and Customs declaration. These are photocopies and you can keep them.'

Linda and Martin devoured the two documents as though they were maps of buried treasure.

Name of Vessel: *Milady*
Date: 7th September
Last Port of Call: Bermuda
Registry: Portsmouth 84/3047
Destination: Lymington
Name of Captain: Eric Glazer/Male/British/
Passport No 36280
Crew: Greta Glazer/Female/British/Pass-
    port No 36281
    Arabella Campbell/USA/Passport
    No 01268C
        Signed — E. Glazer

That was the crew list. The Customs declaration was equally brief.

Name of Vessel: *Milady*
Date: 7 September
Last Port: Bermuda
Destination: Lymington

Then there were four columns: Description of dutiable goods/quantity/value/Duty payable.

Across these had been written: NIL — Small quantity spirits, tobacco and personal possessions only.

Below was also written: No major repairs or alterations abroad. Again it was signed: E. Glazer, Master.

'As far as we were concerned this was a straightforward clearance. We don't have much trouble with these long-distance people. They know the game's not worth the candle. Boats nipping across the Channel sometimes load up with drink or cigarettes — or watches or dope or illegal immigrants — we get everything. It's then we have trouble.'

'Everything was perfectly normal?'

'Yes. The boat had British registry and they showed me the outward Customs clearance. They had taken some duty-free Scotch when they left.'

'How was the boat?'

'It didn't look too bad considering. They'd had a storm halfway across and it had smashed one of the cabin windows. They had a bit of ply fitted over it and screwed down. They asked me about getting a replacement locally.'

'How were the people? Was my sister all right?'

'Well all their passports were in order. In a case like this we do the necessary for British passport holders. The American girl I asked to report to the local police for immigration.'

'And she did?'

'Yes, they sent us confirmation. They'd given her a tourist visa — good for six months. She's not supposed to take work.'

'Did you search the boat?'

'I poked my head into the fo'c'sl and into the after cabin. No reason to do more.'

'Linda,' said Martin holding out one of the forms. 'Would you say that was Eric Glazer's signature? Can we check it?'

'The only letter I've seen was written to Mom by Greta. I suppose we could check it with his firm.'

'I wouldn't go too much on that, Sir,' said Primmer. 'The skipper had hurt his hand in the storm, I remember. It was all tied up. He signed those forms with his left hand, I noticed.'

'Too bad,' said Martin looking disappointed. 'But it probably wouldn't have led to anything.'

'Can you tell us more about the people?' asked Linda. 'Did they seem to be getting on? Were they on good terms? Did my sister seem happy?'

'Happy . . . ' the Inspector let the word hang in the air for a second. 'I'd say so. They all seemed OK. People who've been at sea for a few weeks are glad to get into port — it's an achievement. I sat down and had a cup of coffee with them. They offered me a drink but I don't touch it when I'm on duty. There were three people,' Inspector Primmer went on remembering. 'There was the owner and his wife — both nearly middle-aged. He was medium height and strongly built, she was blonde with a premature touch of grey.'

'Greta didn't have any grey hair, did she Martin?'

'I don't remember any — unless she ran out of peroxide on the crossing. Or the storm gave her some grey hair.'

'The young woman who was crew, your sister that is — she was alive and well. That's all I can say.'

'What's happened? Where is she? Why haven't we heard anything?' Linda, hoping for some dramatic revelation, was disheartened at the normality of everything to do with the yacht's arrival.

'Inspector Primmer,' Martin spoke earnestly. 'So far as we know you're the last person to have seen the yacht and the people on board. Have you any theory — what can have happened? Why haven't we heard from Bella?'

Inspector Primmer pressed his lips together and looked thoughtful.

'I can't tell you, I'm afraid. Since we

knew you were coming we've talked about it. If the boat never turns up the most probable thing is being run down by a big ship at night. But she might be holed up somewhere. They might be sick. Or a letter may have gone astray. So many innocent things can happen. Looking back afterwards you wonder why you worried. Not that you aren't doing right to make enquiries.'

'I sure hope you're right,' Linda said.

'The yacht left a couple of days after that. They didn't have the window replaced in the yard I recommended, so I suppose they meant to do it later. If the boat's in a British yacht harbour there's every chance we'll find her in the end. Her British registry will help.'

'How's that?' Linda asked.

'It's like a car registration. Every registered yacht has a serial number and a registered tonnage and these have to be carved into the main beam or some permanent part of the boat's structure. They are hard to eliminate or disguise.'

'I get it. We've got a system like that in the States,' said Linda. 'But I suppose yacht thieves, like car thieves, could change the number?'

'I'm afraid they could.'

'We're very grateful to you, Inspector. You've given us all the information we could expect,' Martin said.

'I'm sorry I can't tell you more,' the Inspector answered, and turning to Linda, 'I hope you find your sister.'

'Is there anyone else here in Plymouth we ought to contact?'

'You could wander round the docks. There are a few yachts moored here long term with people living on board. They might have talked to your sister or the other two. Yacht people in the same port often get together.'

★ ★ ★

Linda and Martin walked round the docks and talked to three or four owners they found living on boats, but nobody remembered *Milady* or her crew. They went to the Royal Western Yacht Club, scanned the Visitors' Book and talked to a steward who referred them to a bluff, bearded Secretary, but none of it led to anything.

It seemed that *Milady* had come and gone, without leaving any more permanent trace than a boat's hull leaves in its passage through the water.

16

Bloody Business

It was a half-derelict isolated building on the south bank of the Thames in what had once been part of dockland. In the past this, like the north side of the river, had been one of the busiest parts of London — packed with shipping and crowded with stevedores, tallymen, drivers, Customs officials, shipping agents, crews, hawkers, touts, prostitutes and hangers-on of all kinds. Now strikes and go-slows, development of other ports, container handling, mechanisation — all these had combined to create a world of empty warehouses, echoing vaults, ghostly wharves and deserted offices, of which this building was one. There had been some demolition round about and the only business near was a large and very noisy yard where they graded and handled tons of gravel for road building. It was a district shunned even by squatters and winos since there were no nearby shops for the one and no passers-by to beg from for the other. There were plans for redevelopment, but these lagged behind those for north of the river. It would happen some day.

In the meantime a room could be leased for a short term at a low rent — and no questions asked. It was just the sort of office to suit a firm like Southern Traders Company that wanted a secluded site with storage in the cellar and had no need for a fashionable address. Southern Traders was a business that valued privacy and was prepared to put up with insalubrious surroundings so long as it was allowed to get on with the profitable work of distributing its product from a secure centre. In the past few years business had been good. Perhaps things had been too easy. For now there was serious competition from an American rival firm and Southern Traders, certainly at first, had been taken unawares.

In fact two of their most senior executives had been forced to retire from business — permanently. The two men now in the office were the only remaining members of the board of directors and they were expecting a vigorous takeover bid from their rivals. If they could be induced to retire or persuaded to leave the business, the Americans would have a clear field to operate in. Southern Traders were prepared to put up what you could really describe as a fight to the finish. The stakes were high. It meant the control of a profitable part of the European drug market.

Southern Traders' office was well equipped for their purpose. As well as serving as an operating base for day-to-day business, it was designed to outbid any takeover. Besides a good supply and quite a wide range of their stock-in-trade, the office equipment included (though only in case of need) two hand-guns, several grenades and a sawn-off shotgun. The doors had been reinforced and the windows covered with strong iron grilles.

In fact they had already had the good fortune to meet one of the

American opponents reconnoitring outside the building and had been able to convince him that drugs could be a health hazard. Also, when they shot him, the silencer they possessed hadn't even been necessary because of the noise from the gravel factory. Noises inside were likely to draw even less attention.

Besides the man they had shot there were two more of their American rivals down below. All three Americans were off a large motor-yacht which about a week before had come into port and, having properly gone through the formalities, had been able to get a berth in a disused dock on the south side of the river. The older of the two spoke such good English that you could hardly tell he was originally of German origin. He was accompanied by a tough-looking younger man with a New York accent. They both carried guns and the younger one had a flick-knife. They looked down at the body on the ground. It had been abandoned there because Southern Traders had thought it wise to retire to their office without hanging around. The older man said a few words of goodbye to his dead colleague. 'Bloody fool. He would go ahead. He should have waited for us. There are only two of them.'

'How about if they call up buddies?'

'Tiny here took care of the telephone. Anyhow they haven't got that many buddies now — not since we took care of the two big boys.'

'That was a sweet job, boss. Two heavy lumps at the bottom of the river and sure to stay there. How about sending Tiny for a swim too? He's sure had it.'

'We'll fix our pals inside first. He can wait. Drag him over to that pile of junk and get that corrugated sheet over him. Now how are we going to tackle them? You'd better go back to the boat. There's a couple of pineapples hidden away, you know where. And get a torch, the light's going and it could be dark here soon.'

'OK, boss.'

'If Ray's back bring him along — and tell Eva what we're doing.'

'Aren't Ray and his girl taking the small yacht down the coast soon?'

'Yes, and meeting us in France. There's a rendezvous there next week.'

★ ★ ★

Armed with their weapons which now included grenades, they crept up the bare staircase. The building was mostly empty, with bare boards, gaping doors, broken windows and litter on the floors, and they explored hastily. When they got to the third floor the landing and passage had been swept and there was a sign with an arrow, Southern Traders Company. Beyond on the left there was a closed door. The two men stopped and hesitated like hounds fetched up by an obstacle. Then the older man called out: 'Ahoy! Ahoy there! Can we talk? Just a friendly talk. There's no danger. We can arrange things.'

They stood there stockstill, ready to shoot, tense and frozen. The older of the two by some sixth sense had a premonition of danger. Sure enough the door opened a fraction with a sudden shaft of light. There was a hollow rolling sound on the bare passage floor.

'Look out!' Karl shouted and half leapt, half threw himself along the passage and down the stairs, tangling and tumbling with the other man. There was a second's silence, then a shattering explosion, a tearing sound and the noise of falling debris. Dust and small pieces of plaster came down on the two men crouching half-a-flight down the stairs, bruised but otherwise unhurt.

Karl grinned in the growing dark. 'They should have left it another two seconds,' he whispered, 'and they'd have got us. It's hard to wait with the thing in your hand.'

They stayed there listening to see if the noise would raise a hue and cry, but if anyone heard the explosion, nobody seemed anxious to investigate.

Again Karl spoke low to his companion: 'I'm going up on the roof. I'll take the grenades and the torch. Keep an eye on the door and shoot if they come out. Be ready to duck down the stairs again if they throw anything.'

He picked up some pieces of plaster

dislodged by the explosion and crept up the stairs, past the scarred passage, then climbed another flight which brought him out on to a flat roof. First he looked over the parapet down to the floor below fixing the whereabouts of the one lighted window and noting the heavy grille over it. Then he went over to the chimney above the lighted room and climbed up so he could lean over the top of it.

Above the brickwork of the chimney, four chimney-pots projected, set square like the dots on number-four dice. They were obviously for different flues from different fireplaces down below, but there was no means of knowing which was which. Listening carefully, Karl started to drop pieces of plaster down each of the red-clay chimney-pots. At the third one he heard the plaster drop and to confirm it was the right room there came a shot.

'Aha, they don't believe in Father Christmas,' he thought, 'well, here's a Christmas cracker. About a second to drop.'

Taking a grenade from his pocket he

held it over the chimney pot and bending his head and body down pulled out the pin by feel and let the lever go, counting as he still held it — One . . . two . . . three . . . four . . . and let go. The grenade was timed to go off five seconds after release. He had gauged it exactly.

There was a muffled explosion and some indistinguishable sounds came up. He understood why the first bang had not attracted attention, as it was not nearly so loud from outside. So he had the less hesitation in repeating the operation with a second grenade. One . . . two . . . three . . . four . . . This time following the explosion no sound came up. Karl nodded his head and went down to the other man.

'You sure blew 'em up, boss,' he was greeted with admiration.

'Hmph. We'd better go and have a look.'

It took them some time to get through the door. When they started there was someone groaning inside but by the time they got in the sound had stopped. They found a medium-sized room, badly wrecked by the explosions, and two bodies. The place had never been modernised and the open grate with a portable electric fire in front of it had not stopped the full force of the grenade blast. One body lay on its face with a hole in the head, oozing blood. The other with eyes open and face muscles stretched in a grin of agony, had no visible wound until Karl rolled it over with his foot and they saw a wound had been blown in the small of the back. Like professional butchers they were unmoved by the shambles and set to work at once, searching the room for the immediate reward — a stock of drugs.

'We can leave these boys. They might have blown themselves up. Can you get into the safe?'

'Not me boss. Tiny was the expert. An' he's lying quiet down below.'

However, they found keys undamaged in one of the dead men's pockets, and one of these fitted the safe. It was three-quarters full of packages. Karl opened samples and tried them with an expert eye and tongue. 'Barbs, coke and snuff — might be dionin or heroin. Not bad.

Say fifteen thousand quid at current rates — our new rates, eh. Now there's plenty to do. Get Tiny's body into the drink. We need some bags to shift this stuff. We'll leave some behind and lock the safe. And there's got to be another stack of stuff down in the cellar according to my information. That'll be another of the keys. We'll get Eva to help us.'

'OK, boss.'

'Go easy too and keep your eyes open. There might be someone on the lookout after all that noise.'

17

Hatton Garden and Scotland Yard

Van Loon and Bonnet had offices at the far end of Hatton Garden beyond the diamond dealers and jewellery shops. They had been dealers in precious stones, but now most of their business was in *objets d'art*. They had offices in Amsterdam and Paris as well as in London. In addition to the phone call from Linda, Paula had written from America, and when Pieter van Loon returned from abroad he phoned the Club on Monday and suggested they see him on Tuesday afternoon. They spent Monday sightseeing, then on Tuesday after an Italian lunch in Soho, they strolled along Piccadilly in the afternoon sunshine, Linda almost feeling she was becoming a settled Londoner. The oak-panelled room they were shown into was as much like a private study as an office and Pieter van Loon was as welcoming as his surroundings were elegant.

'How do you do? You're Mrs Campbell's daughter?' He shook hands. 'And Mr Firth — Mrs Campbell called you Martin. Welcome both of you.'

'Mother thought you might be able to help us,' said Linda.

'I'll be only too glad to help you or your mother. Not only is she one of our regular customers, but I have a high regard for her — both personally and as a collector. I was sorry to read the news in your mother's letter. Tell me the whole story.'

He listened sympathetically while they went over the disappearance of Bella and the yacht. His interest became more professional when Linda described the circumstances of the burglary. Then he concentrated his fullest attention when she gave details of the missing pieces.

'That's what was lost,' she finished. 'Maybe there's less point enquiring here than in the States. But we thought we ought to let you know.'

'Yes. I'm very glad you have. We

handled the sale of two of those items to your mother, the Limoges grisaille and one of the English snuff-boxes. Did you bring descriptions or photographs?'

'We've got descriptions and measurements but not photos I'm afraid.'

'We might have photos on our files, though it's some time ago. I remember the sale of the Limoges. Your enquiries may not be as pointless as you think. Art theft is an international crime. Usually the loot travels the other way, from Europe to America — but you never know. Of course it was all insured?'

'Yes,' said Martin. 'I've been working for the same insurance company, Golden Eagle, but I didn't handle the loss claim. I'm in the marine insurance division. In broad outline, Mrs Campbell will get more than the enamels cost but not as much as the things are worth by present-day market value. There's a reward for information leading to their recovery, if that's any inducement.'

'It might be better to keep the reward quiet for the moment,' said Pieter. 'It would let the thieves know that we're searching in this part of the world. What I suggest is this. Our firm can cast a pretty wide net. We could advise dealers that we have a client, an Australian say, who is looking for antiques in a range that would include your mother's missing items. The thieves might well have offered them to a reputable dealer — especially in another part of the world. Dealers try to check the *bona fides* of people they buy from, but enquiries can be pretty casual. Something might be on sale.'

'That would be great. If we can get anything back Mom would be delighted. Of course finding Bella is the most important but you never know, maybe the two were connected and it was the Glazers who took them.'

'I'll let you know if anything comes of it. We might not get names and addresses out of the dealers. There's a lot of confidentiality in this business. We might trace the pieces but not the people who stole them — even if you brought the police in.'

'That would still be worth while. We're very grateful.'

'Good luck with your other enquiries. I hope you enjoy your holiday as far as possible. Can I get you tickets for anything or arrange any sightseeing?'

'No, it's all right, thank you,' said Martin. 'My parents live in Hampshire and I know London well enough.'

'Well, I hope to be in touch. Be sure to give your mother my good wishes when you write.'

★ ★ ★

Before Linda and Martin called at Scotland Yard a letter with another one enclosed arrived from Drew. He wrote:

My Dear Poppet, Your Dad thinks of you in Old England and hopes the search for the missing one is going apace. I expect you'll have met Martin's folks, give them our best wishes and hope to see them over here at a future date. I hope you see some sights too and perhaps visit Bonnie Scotland where my forebears hail from though I haven't had it all traced. The main reason for writing is to send on a letter I got about our guests Eric and Greta that shows my suspicions about them were right. It turns out that they aren't as we thought truly English, but he was a refugee who came over from Germany in the 1930s. Also he was retired and not actually working for the company as we thought. I just hope you can catch up with the yacht and rescue Bella from their clutches. All the folk at the sailing club send everything to you and Martin, and Paula joins me in a big hug and kisses — from Your Dad.

The letter enclosed was from the Personnel Manager of the Kaufman Pure Drug Company and read as follows:

Dear Mr Campbell — I am replying to your letter enquiring about the status of Mr Eric Glazer and whether he is in fact an employee of our firm. I understand your concern for your daughter and sincerely hope her silence may have some innocent cause. Under the circumstances I am happy to answer your questions, though I fear I can say little to throw light on the matter.

Mr Glazer worked for us for over ten years and was currently on extended leave prior to retirement. He came to us from another pharmaceutical firm and was especially useful because of his German background. He was brought up in Germany and came to England at the time of the Nazi regime. The combination of laboratory experience and knowledge of language made him very valuable to us after the war, both in Germany and other countries. I hope you will treat this as confidential since he was a naturalised British subject, they had both settled in England, made friends here, spoke without foreign accents and I think wished to forget their German origins.

Since he went on the cruise, Mr Glazer wrote from the West Indies to a colleague in the firm and sent a postcard from America, but none of us has heard from him since. We have no address other than their house in

Hampshire which I understand is still in the hands of agents. The Glazers had no children and our records give as next-of-kin a cousin living in Tel Aviv.

Again I hope you will soon hear from your daughter.

Yours sincerely, Paul Smyth, Personnel.

'What do you think of that?' asked Linda when Martin had read the two letters.

'One thing looks certain — there won't be many people looking for the Glazers and there's only us looking for Bella. Once people go on a long cruise they drop out of circulation.'

'The Glazers seemed such an ordinary middle-class couple to me. He obviously had had a respectable job and we know they had a country house and a boat. I don't see them as art thieves. Didn't they strike you as typical?'

'Yes they definitely did — typically English I'd say. We talked about sailing over here and Glazer mentioned one chap in the Lymington Club that I had actually met racing. But I suppose respectable people *might* be tempted if they saw something very easy.'

'Pop's got these prejudices about anyone with a foreign background. Maybe Bella took Mom's things. It would account for a lot.'

'Surely not. She had money for her stay here and her passage back, didn't she?'

'Yes, she'd have enough, but not too much. Pop was reasonable but he didn't chuck it about. I shouldn't say this of my sister, but she did have an acquisitive streak and she wanted things in a big way. She was really struck with Ramón and the way he spread money around apparently regardless. And recently she didn't confide in me at all. She was determined to go her own way, and she always had a reckless streak in her too. Bella and I had really drifted apart in the days before she left. As I've said, I'm sure she was on drugs and I think it affected her.'

'Well, I don't know,' said Martin, running his hand through his hair.

'Anything's possible. All we can do is keep asking and hope something will turn up.'

'This is your sister's report form,' said Inspector Donald to Linda and Martin as they sat in an office in the large modern building now housing Scotland Yard. 'We got this information two weeks ago through Interpol. Would you just look through it to see that all the details are correct.'

The form carried a photo of Bella with full personal details such as age, race, complexion, height, weight, etc, etc. There followed particulars of the circumstances: Left Bermuda as crew on 30-foot ketch *Milady*, British Registry, Portsmouth 84/3047, with owner & wife E. Glazer. Yacht cleared Customs Plymouth 7th Sept., three crew well. Left again, destination Lymington, without making coastguard report. No contact yacht or crew since.

'Well,' said Linda impressed. 'It's very

detailed. What's a coastguard report?'

'Yachtsmen leaving port can send particulars of the boat and the voyage to the coastguard service, and then tell their family or a friend when they expect to arrive. If they don't turn up the friend will get in touch with the nearest coastguard station who can organise a search knowing just what they're looking for. I'm afraid on a short coastal passage a lot of yachtsmen don't bother.'

'Inspector Donald, from your experience, have you any idea what might have happened?'

'Have you thought your sister might have dropped out of sight deliberately?'

'I don't know. She and Poppa didn't hit it off sometimes. He can be the real old-fashioned father, and Bella was a bit wild. But it wasn't too serious.'

'I just mention it because there are plenty of cases of young people leaving home, husbands leaving wives and vice versa who are reported as missing persons. And they've gone because they wanted to live their own lives. Unless there's a suggestion of accident or crime or suicide, we don't carry out a search. Except for children. And if we come across a person who doesn't want their whereabouts known, we tell the family they are well but we're not entitled to disclose where they are.'

'You mean if you knew where Bella was you wouldn't tell me — her sister?'

'Not if she was all right and didn't want you to know.'

'But we're worried about her.'

'That's another matter. In a case like this where there might have been an accident to the yacht, we do all we can. All these particulars go on a computer that covers this country and abroad — police stations as well as coastguard. And so far there's nothing.'

'We'll just have to keep on hoping. At least you've shown us how comprehensive the system is.'

'That's right, don't give up hope. You'd be surprised how many people turn up with some innocent reason for having been out of touch. We'll certainly let you know if we get any information.'

18

Stolen Goods

After their Scotland Yard interview, Linda and Martin seemed to have come to the end of all they could do by way of detective work. They had talked to the authorities, they had followed up all the leads. The sum of everything was that they had got exactly nowhere.

'This never happened to all those famous detectives,' said Linda glumly as they sat lunching in a Chinese restaurant courageously eating *dim sum* with chopsticks.

'Depends which famous detectives you mean,' said Martin. 'I'll bet it never happened to Sexton Blake or Double-o-seven (if you can call him a detective). It might have happened to Dixon of Dock Green — but only temporarily.'

'You know it's most unfair. You're managing your chopsticks a lot better than I'm doing. How do you do it?'

'I got a lesson from a Chinese client who took me out to lunch. Now he's got a boat in Singapore that we insure. You have to hold the end of the chopstick under your thumb and then put it between the first and second finger, like this . . . '

'Oh yes . . . I see . . . it works! That makes everything easier. Oh bother, I've dropped a bit. This *tofu* is too soft to pick up.'

Martin smiled at his wife indulgently, amused at her battle with the chopsticks.

'What are we going to do? — to get back to business,' Linda went on. 'Go into the country and stay with your folks? You don't go back to work for a time yet.'

'If we went down to Hampshire, we'd be near the Glazers' house. We could talk to the Estate Agents or we might find friends or neighbours who could tell us something. You know, when I start work, we'll also have to find somewhere to live. If I'm based in Hampshire we could start house-hunting.'

'Our own place,' Linda enthused. 'Even if it's only two rooms and a double bed. Where will it be?'

'Head office is in London. But they've got three branches I might go to — Portsmouth, York or Glasgow. I'm hoping this Baltimore job will turn up eventually, so nothing's too permanent.'

'I don't mind where we go really. What I've seen of England so far is just OK — I mean — *all right.*'

'Congratulations, darling, you're picking up English *real fast*,' Martin teased her. 'To come back to what we are going to do. Why not wait another day? It's always darkest before the dawn.'

'Yes I know. 'There is a budding morrow in midnight.' 'If Winter comes, can Spring be far behind?' You learn these quotes at school as another boring chore — then as time goes on you realise that besides sounding good, they happen to be *true*. All right, another day, then. A yacht and three people can't just vanish into thin air.'

* * *

The accumulated wisdom of the generations turned out to be right. The next day they were out visiting the Kennedy Memorial at Runnymead, but on their return there was a message from Pieter van Loon: 'Come And See Me As Soon As You Can. I Have Some Information That May Help You.'

Full of anticipation, they arrived at van Loon and Bonnet's early next morning. Pieter was engaged and they had half-an-hour's wait.

'I'm sorry you had to wait,' he said. 'But it's something worth waiting for. I think — just *think* — I may have found one of your mother's pieces.'

'No, really? That's great!' exclaimed Linda.

Pieter looked through a tray on his desk, found a letter and a photograph clipped together and handed them the photo to look at.

'This was sent yesterday by our Paris office. It came from another French antiques firm, Jean Fourneaux. I told you we had handled two of the pieces your mother lost, one of them being a

Limoges enamel 17th century. I looked for a photo on our files but it was seven years ago your mother bought it and we only keep detailed records for five years. However, from what I remember this looks very like it. What do you think?'

'It's mother's,' said Linda, 'I'd swear to it.'

'They say in this letter that the plaque belonged to a French family from Touraine, the present owner is living in England, the asking price is twenty thousand dollars and the owner doesn't want the plaque to leave Europe. I suspect that means the owner doesn't want to sell to an American, which might or might not be suspicious. If it's the one that was stolen and it then ended in an American collection it might be recognised.'

'What can we do?'

'Go to Paris and see Jean Fourneaux. They are holding the plaque and you'd have to see it. You can't be sure from a photo. If you're sure you can identify it, you could tell Fourneaux it's stolen and go to the French police. Our Paris office would help you.'

'I see.'

'But you might not be able to trace the thieves or get the other stolen items back. These people are expert at covering their tracks and using accommodation addresses.'

'That would be a pity.'

'If you want to appear genuine buyers and need a cover story, I could tell them you are buying for an Australian insurance company. You might ask for the owner's address, but again you might have trouble getting it, but there's a chance. Do you want to go to Paris?'

Martin and Linda looked at one another.

'Do we want to go to Paris? A couple of days in Paris would be wonderful!' Linda exclaimed.

'Indeed they would,' Martin confirmed. 'We can go right away. We'd like to use the cover story you suggest, wouldn't we Linda?'

'Yes, we would. It's a marvellous find. Last night we were right at the bottom of the barrel. I don't know how we can thank you.'

'That's all right. I'll ring up our Paris office now.' He dialled. '*Monsieur Bonnet? Henri . . . les jeunes mariés,* Linda *et* Martin Firth. *Ils veulent voir la plaque chez Fourneaux en passant chez vous auparavant. Pourriez-vous prévenir Paul chez Fourneaux? Dites lui qu'ils achètent pour une compagnie d'assurance australienne. Est-ce que demain vous conviendra? A quelle heure? Vers la fin de l'aprèsmidi. Oui. Oui. Bon, d'accord. Merci. Au revoir.*'

'There. My colleague Henri Bonnet will expect you tomorrow afternoon. Bon voyage. Let me know how you get on.'

* * *

The offices of Jean Fourneaux were in the Champs Elysées. They had an appointment to see a Monsieur Paul Duchamp the morning after their arrival in Paris. This had been arranged for them the previous afternoon by Pieter's colleague, Henri Bonnet. Making an early start from London they had arrived at the Gare du Nord by noon in good time to book into a hotel and wander along the Seine to van Loon and Bonnet's office. They had even been able to go to a show and find an excellent restaurant afterwards for supper. Now as they walked up the Champs Elysées in wintery, mid-morning sunshine, they felt that Paris was treating them well.

'Once we're sure it's Mom's Limoges plaque it's important to get the address of the seller,' said Linda.

'Without them knowing, if possible.'

'He's bound to have it on his desk.'

'If we can distract his attention.'

'We'll have to see how things turn out,' Linda concluded.

★ ★ ★

Paul Duchamp was square and broad-shouldered, but though he looked capable of handling bricks or sacks of coal, his movements were delicate as a cat and his hands fluttered over the papers on his desk as lightly as a woman's. Preliminary introductions and greetings over — *enchanté Madame, Monsieur* — he asked them if they spoke French.

'*Très peu*,' Martin replied, '*Plutôt . . . j'aimerais mieux* — that is — er . . . '

'*Alors*. Let us talk English. I can enough for business.'

'You have heard from Monsieur Bonnet about my colleague and me,' said Martin. 'We are interested in this antique plaque for my company as an investment. May we see it please.'

'*Oui*, naturally. I will get it from the strong-room and we can look shortly. Anyone from van Loon and Bonnet . . . ' he spread his hands, 'is welcome. Of course you know the price.'

'Perhaps we can discuss later. Will we be able to meet the owner?'

'*Malheureusement* — he does not want to appear. We have authority.'

'Can you give us his name — address perhaps? Or is he a she — a woman?'

Monsieur Duchamp smiled, and fingered a letter on his desk. 'That too is impossible. You know our clients are rich. They do not want to be bothered — press, publicity, charities. They need a screen. We are not just salesmen, no.'

'I see. Perhaps it doesn't matter. Can we see the plaque now? Perhaps you will go and get it? We can wait here,' said Martin, hoping to be left alone with the letter on the desk.

'Yes, I will have it brought in,' Paul Duchamp touched a bell on his desk.

'What a fine office,' remarked Linda. 'You have such a splendid view. You can see the Champs Elysées and you even get a glimpse of the Seine.' Trying another ploy to get Paul Duchamp away from the desk, Linda went over to one of the windows.

'A fine view. From that window is best,' he agreed. But he did not move and in any case a girl came into the office without delay.

'*Annique, prenez les clés. Monsieur et Madame s'intéréssent à l'émail de Limoges. Apportez-le ici, s'il vous plaît.*'

Annique returned in a few minutes with the enamel. Martin had seen over Paula's collection, but he didn't remember this particular piece and he gazed at it now in genuine admiration. It illustrated the traditional story of Saint Christopher and it showed him carrying the Christ child across a river. The figures were small but perfectly drawn in grisaille — light grey with a grey-and-white background. On the grey hill were grey trees, in the river ran grey water and there swam tiny grey fish. The only relief was provided by the haloes that floated over the heads of the two figures and these were touched lightly with gold. It was strange and sad, but an object of great beauty.

'What an unusual thing,' said Linda. 'May I look at it?' She picked it up and turned it over, looking carefully at the back, seeming as interested in that as in the front.

'*Le couleur* — the grey was something very new at the time,' Duchamp explained. 'And it became famous. Like the blue of Wedgwood you know.'

'May I take a photo?' Martin asked. 'I have my camera. It will help when we get back to London. I may have to send an appraiser but this would help.'

'Of course. How do you want it? Just on the desk — here?'

'That's fine,' said Martin and took

several rapid flashlight shots. 'It really is a fine piece. There is one last thing — Monsieur Duchamp — the price. Twenty thousand is a lot. Would the owner consider an offer?'

'For nowadays it is reasonable. We had a grisaille six months ago, slightly larger but not so interesting. It went for twenty-one. That was at an auction so because of the publicity and the competition the price might have gone higher. The owner wants to sell this privately so might accept less. So — a near offer perhaps.'

Soon they left with mutual compliments and good wishes, a promise that Martin would have first refusal as against any other buyer and a promise from Martin that he would be in touch within a week.

'Are they really from an Australian company?' said Duchamp to himself after they had gone. 'He was English and she was American. It's only America the owners object to — they won't mind Australia. Oh well,' he shrugged. '*Pourvu qu'ils avient l'argent.*'

187

'It's mother's plaque all right,' burst out Linda, her eyes bright with excitement, when they were back out on the street. 'There were some initials and a date on the back that tally. Oh damn, damn, why couldn't we get the address of the owner? You tried and I tried but nothing worked. Were they suspicious or are we dud amateurs?'

'Just dealers' caution I expect,' said Martin with a grin.

'What we wanted was a good French detective — Maigret or Gaboriau's Monsieur Lecoq. They'd have thought of something.'

'Well I did think of something. With a bit of luck I may actually have the owner's address,' said Martin a trifle smug.

'How? How?' Linda challenged him.

'In the camera . . . For two of the snaps I held the camera high enough to get in the letter that was lying on Duchamp's desk. The enamel was just next to it.'

'That's great! Oh, darling, you're a genius! Then let's have a grand meal this evening to celebrate — or do we have to rush back to England?'

'Let's do both — like Nelson.'

'You mean Drake, of course,' Linda corrected him. 'Do we go to the police in the meantime?'

'I think it's more important to trace the owner on the QT if we can. If we make a big fuss and claim the plaque as stolen property now, the owner will disappear. We can always go to the police later.'

'All right, I agree.'

19

Boat Yard

An express developing service in London gave them prints of Martin's photo within a few hours. The print of the letter was clear, but it was too small to be decipherable so they asked for an enlargement. Then they got a further blow-up of the parts which showed the letter-head with the address, and also the name at the bottom. The costs mounted, but with these second enlargements they were able to read an address at the head of the letter, though the results for the signature and the name of the signatory at the foot of the letter were disappointing as this part of Martin's original snapshot was slightly out of focus. The signature itself was quite unreadable and the name under it looked like Poster or Easter. There was no doubt however, about the address. It was Frank Foster & Son,

27 Wherry Lane, Falmouth, Cornwall. Poster and Easter were evidently out-of-focus versions of Foster. The letter was in English and its contents, so far as they could make them out, told them nothing they didn't already know.

'We've got to go down to Cornwall,' said Linda.

'I agree. It is a port so we seem to be getting warmer. At last we've got an address.'

The next day they left the Club, took the train again and by evening were booked into a bed-and-breakfast place in the seaside town.

★ ★ ★

Wherry Lane was down near the waterfront, but there was no view of the water or any atmosphere of boats or of the seaside. The dingy road was shut in on both sides by buildings, walls and fences, black with age and crumbling with neglect. There could hardly be an unlikelier place for the owner, even the illegal owner, of valuable antiques. Linda and Martin walked along with rising doubts, expecting perhaps to discover some dilapidated old curiosity shop, but when they came to number 27 all they found was a yard and some buildings hidden behind a high fence with a heavy gate, shut and massively padlocked, and with a worn name and number painted on it. The gate simply ignored Martin's pushing and there was no response to their hammering or to their shouting through the letter box opening. They tried enquiring at other places along the road.

'Number 27? It's a boat repair yard,' they were told at a warehouse. 'Closed? I wouldn't know. I think it changed hands recently. You could try telephoning.'

A little tobacco-sweet-provision shop on the corner knew no more: 'One of the chaps from Fosters used to come in for fags, but I haven't seen him for six months. A lot of these small firms pack up — the taxes get them.' From a local telephone box they tried a number they got from Directory Enquiries, but there was no reply.

'What do we do now?' asked Linda over a cup of tea. 'Stay the night here and try tomorrow? Or give up and go back to London?'

'I'm damned if I'll give up after getting so far,' said Martin stubbornly. 'I'm going to get over that fence somehow. The address was as clear as a bell and the letter was about selling your mother's enamel. This might be their day off or they're only there part time.'

'You don't mean break in — at night? Robin Hood stuff? I suppose being you, you do. It means we give up making love in a nice warm bed too. That wasn't what I got married for.'

'Nor me neither, darling. Not no-how. Though they're only rather creaky singles with thin mattresses.'

'Yes, there is that. I suppose one night won't hurt us. You're sure it's worth it?'

'I think so. If they've got something to hide we've got a better chance of finding it out, when the place is empty. What do we need? We're dressed casually and we can change into trainers. We need a good torch, a bit of rope, a strip of metal we can bend into a hook — then a dark night and a certain amount of luck. OK?'

'Well ye-es, all right, honey. It's certainly taking the bull by the horns. I guess it's better than just waiting around. The chances are that Frank Foster has been taken over by E & G Glazer or else the place is a cover for some art gang. Either way we get somewhere.'

They went back to the undistinguished lodging-house where they had been staying and booked in for a second night. From a friendly ironmonger they were able to buy a torch, twelve feet of nylon line and an inch-wide strip of strong metal that could be bent into a hook. It cost them another pound to have a hole drilled in the metal so they could fix it to the rope. Fortunately the ironmonger was used to doing odd jobs for sailing enthusiasts so he made no demur about drilling the hole, when they told him it was part of a new experimental, self-steering gadget.

In the evening having made their purchases, they found a fish restaurant on the quay. It was offering lobster, crabs and enormous mussels and they were treated to a meal every bit as good as anything they had had in Paris.

'Let's do ourselves well and have a decent meal,' said Linda half jokingly. 'If there's some art gang in there and they start shooting it might be our last one.'

'It might be our last one in England as good as this anyway,' said Martin. 'With all Europe wanting to fish in these waters we might be better off soon in the Chesapeake.'

'Dearth or death eh,' said Linda.

'Let's hope we find nobody in the yard and plenty of clues to lead us to Bella safe and sound. We want clues too that we can hand over to the police. I think this ought to be the last time we go in for this do-it-yourself lark. What do you think?'

'I'm with you a hundred per cent,' said Linda.

Later in the evening they went back to the boarding-house. They put on their trainers and packed up the rest of their things in a suitcase. They left this in the room and got out of the boarding-house without attracting attention, just before midnight. They took with them passports, papers and money, just in case of trouble, and the things they had bought at the ironmongers. A moon was due to come up about two and the tide would be high at six-thirty. Sunrise was not until seven-thirty. But by seven it would be light enough to see.

'Even if we need daylight to see anything, we must be out of the place by seven-thirty,' said Martin.

The town was quiet and as they got down near the harbour the streets were virtually deserted. Dressed as they were, they might well be a yachting couple going back to their boat. In Wherry Lane there was not a soul. Setting Linda to keep watch, Martin unpacked the rope and the strip of metal which was now bent into a broad hook, and tied it on with a bowline. He had got it ready beforehand in the privacy of the bedroom of their lodgings.

The fence was some seven or eight feet high, but it was not protected by spikes or netting. With the rope coiled in his left hand, Martin swung the end with his right hand, and threw the hook up and over, his experience of throwing ropes from boats helping him. He thought he should have padded the hook with cloth, but in the circumstances he reckoned a little clatter would hardly be noticed. At the third cast the hook caught on top of the fence at the strongest part near the gatepost. He called softly to Linda.

'I'll go first,' he said in an undertone, 'in case there's someone inside. I can pull you up after me. It's no harder than going up a mast.'

'No bosun's chair though. But then what's seven feet,' Linda whispered back.

'Right.' Martin gripped the rope, pulled himself up, got a hand on the fence, then a foot over and he was astride.

'It's all quiet this side,' he called softly. 'OK, come up.'

Half climbing, half pulled, Linda was soon beside him. They dropped down easily the other side on to a pile of timber that came halfway up the fence. In the street behind them and in the yard beside them all was quiet. But now they were over the fence they could hear faint noises of boats and water coming from the harbour. Somewhere very gently there was the sharp persistent tattoo of a halyard tap-tap-tapping against a hollow metal mast. A dim glow came from an overhead light nearer the water and also from a solitary street-lamp in the lane behind them. Around them in dark shapes and shadows they could see piles of materials, used timber and old iron, boats on props and cradles, the arm of a crane, a winch, the hollow mouth of a shed — all the purposeful clatter associated with marine building and repair.

'Frank Foster and Son, eh?' whispered Martin, 'Now it's Eric Glazer and Company for sure. Come on, let's explore.'

They left the rope and hook near the wall and, holding the torch, Martin led the way between the various obstacles. They came to a building and peered through a window. With the help of the torch they could make out a desk, chairs, a typewriter — it was evidently an office.

'We ought to explore inside,' said Linda. 'But it's locked.'

They got in by finding they could force one of the windows. Once inside they went through the desk and a filing cabinet beside it, but all the letters, invoices and account books seemed to be genuinely concerned with boat repairs or the supply of equipment, the provision of moorings, services or yacht agency. A second room with a sink and an Ascot had cutlery, crockery, an electric kettle and some snacks. Another room at the back was fitted up as a store with shelving. There were chrome fittings, fastenings, boat parts, coils of rope. A loft ladder led to a room running the whole length of the building where there were fibre-glass dinghy moulds and small repairs had evidently been carried out. Big barn doors and a hoist at one end gave access and a means of lifting heavy objects in or out. There seemed nothing suspicious or unusual.

They went back to the first room that

was the office. There was a small safe, a key-board with keys on it, and a second cupboard that seemed empty.

'I'd like to get into that safe,' Martin grumbled, 'We might find the rest of Paula's stolen enamels.'

'We ought to go down and have a look at the boats before it's light,' suggested Linda. 'That key-board has got keys with names that look like boats. It wouldn't have *Milady* there by any chance?'

But though they ran through the names *Milady* was not among them.

Then Martin, fossicking about in the empty second cupboard, made a sudden exclamation — 'Look, look at this!' He came over with a small plastic package. 'This was under a newspaper at the bottom of the cupboard. What do you reckon it is?'

'It looks like tobacco,' said Linda doubtfully, fingering the brown shreds.

'It's marijuana. Neither of us is into drugs but I can recognise this. This is the stuff they smoke at those college sessions when they pass round the occasional joint — grass, dope. I reckon the cupboard's been full of it.'

'Yes, I've had a puff, just to be matey,' Linda admitted. 'They looked like badly-rolled cigarettes. It never had any effect on me.'

'It's pretty mild as drugs go unless you smoke a lot of it. Let's have another look.' From the back of a higher shelf he found some brown caked powder and from another shelf he picked up some white grains on his moistened finger.

'There you are, those are both stronger — and the cost goes up accordingly, I'm told. The brown powder's hash — cannabis is another name — and old writers knew it as bhang. Ever read the *Count of Monte Cristo?* It was bhang that gave the hero strange dreams after he escaped from prison and began a new life. And I'm not sure, but I reckon those white grains are coke. You sniff it and, man, as they say, does it sharpen you up.'

'It's not the sort of thing you expect to find in a boat-yard,' said Linda. 'Boats and drugs. I've a feeling we're on to something — boats, drugs and Paula's enamels. Isn't it all beginning to come together? Here, come and have a quick cup of tea. I've found some biscuits. Then we can go and look at the boats.'

They left the building and picked their way down past a slipway sloping in to the water. Here they were now facing the harbour and standing on a stone-faced sea wall with a wooden jetty running out of it. Alongside the jetty were moored four boats: an open work-boat with a boxed engine set near the stern, a large motor cabin-cruiser, a dragon boat with a canvas cover clipped over the cockpit, and finally there was a larger, two-masted yacht, ketch rigged, the main and mizzen sails bent on ready to be hoisted. They crept down the jetty to have a closer look.

'Look! Look at that!'

'Sh . . . sh,' came from Martin. In her excitement Linda had raised her voice, but luckily there was no one to hear.

'Look at that boat. Isn't it — isn't it *Milady*?

20

Drug Addicts and Stowaways

The couple shuffling along Shaftesbury Avenue looked to be in their forties. In fact the man was twenty-eight, the woman only twenty-five. They had both lost the bright bloom of youth in their looks and manner. It was partly their unkempt appearance and shabby dress, partly lack of exercise and general unfitness, but mainly because they had both been heavily on drugs for a long time. At the present moment they were wandering about the town together, hoping desperately to get a fix of some kind.

'I suppose you're right out of everything,' said the man. 'I haven't had a bloody thing for the whole of yesterday. I had some drinks last night, but my patch was a desert for the hard stuff. They've raided a couple of places recently.'

'Yesterday I didn't have sod all either. I've been craving something since last night,' said the woman.

'Well we better see what we can do.'

'How much bread have you got?'

'Only enough for some amps or barbs.'

'That's not going to go far.'

'I knocked off two radios and I've got them in reserve. I tried for a video, but no frigging dice.'

'Two — you might get thirty quid for them if you're lucky. Maybe we could get some coke too. Charlie would give you some tick on the radios.'

'I'll have a damned good frigging try. You'll have to wait around while I go and see Charlie. He don't like more than one customer going in at a time.'

'Here, you better take this. I got nearly ten quid this morning begging on the corner down the road. I reckon it's better than in the tube and less hassle.'

When they met later on a bench in Leicester Square, the man looked a trifle less grey. A heroin injection in the nearest public lavatory had temporarily quietened the worm that was gnawing inside him.

'I got some heroin — and some hash,' he told her. 'Things are no frigging good. Charlie hasn't got much and it's sky high. He gave me some credit. I asked about ecstasy too, but he's right out. There's been a run by kids.'

'Well gimme something. God I need a fix.'

'Here's some speed. Take some of these for now.'

'Ta. God that's better. Anyway what's the trouble?'

'There's a new mob in town and there's aggro all over the place. Thing's ain't settled down yet. Charlie says they're a hard bunch.'

'If I dodge the regulars, I reckon I could go on the batter. The town's swarming with tourists ready to take you to their place. There's nothing like it for a quick turnover. I still got one decent dress.'

'The social worker won't like that.'

'Fuck the social worker, silly old cow. Anyway she won't know.'

'Yeah, but you bloody have to put up a show. She's good for some bread isn't she? Maybe she could get you some dope at the clinic. You know Sheila pulled a line and got three shots a week. Addiction therapy — my foot.'

'Yeah there is that.'

'Charlie had some LSD.'

'Did you get any?'

'I didn't get sod all of anything really. Not even with what I had and pledging the money from the radios. Besides I had a bad trip last time with LSD.'

'God I feel better. I needed those amps.'

'Come on let's go. I got enough still for a drink and a smoke.'

They shuffled off together into their twilight world without much hope for the future, their lives centred on where their next drugs would come from. They were partly protected, partly indulged, partly admonished by the social services, who found them an ongoing problem. Realistically they were likely to get deeper and deeper into crime — begging, theft, prostitution, shop-lifting, fraud.

★ ★ ★

Linda and Martin looked at each other in amazement, doubt, excitement.

'It is *Milady*.'

'Is it? *Milady* was dark blue with light blue topsides. This is all green.'

'There's such a thing as repainting.'

'She's called,' Martin shone a torch discreetly on to the stern '*Angélique*, Brest.'

'And renaming.'

'Supposing we try an experiment,' Martin scraped a tiny spot of the green paint with a pocket-knife. 'There we are, light blue underneath. But the cabin-top didn't go forward of the mast like that. And there wasn't that big spray-guard forward of the cockpit.'

'They could have been added.'

'You're right. Here, you can see where the wood's been scarfed on to extend the cabin-top. I'll bet if we get inside we'll find that the extension is false and that the old deck is still there.

'There was a key marked *Angélique* in the office. Let's get it and have a look inside.'

'If it is *Milady*,' mused Martin. 'No

wonder we were fooled and the authorities found no trace. The Glazers reported they were going east from Plymouth to Lymington, but they went west. It looks as though they were into drugs in a big way. Pop was right. How they took us all in. I wonder why they changed the boat? Perhaps it's because they want to bring in drugs from France. Something else I've just seen. That window's been mended. Remember they broke a window on the way over? In a storm.'

The key from the key-board fitted the door to the cabin and let them in. They undid the forward hatch then relocked the cabin door and returned the key to the office. Now they could leave quickly if necessary by the forward hatch and anyone coming on board would simply suppose that somebody had forgotten to bolt the hatch.

'There's no doubt it's *Milady* all right,' said Linda looking round. I remember the layout of the cabin and that chip on the enamel of the cooker.'

'What about the registered number they gave us. It was 843 . . . something.'

'They said it would be on a big beam near the mast, part of the integral structure. Great Indian chief! It's gone. There's a new number at the side.'

'It's been filled in and painted over,' said Martin, scraping a square millimetre with his knife. 'Easy enough.'

'That's new,' Linda pointed to a gleaming, brand-new ship-to-shore radio-telephone that had been installed over the chart table. Well what do we do?'

'I'd like to go over this in daylight to look for clues. But I think we ought to get out. It's starting to get light and the tide's turning. I think it is a job for the police now. If we stick around too long we might get caught. Eric and Greta aren't going to be crazy to welcome old friends.'

'We might finish up being held in some hide-out along with Bella. Wherever she is.'

'Right. We go and report a stolen yacht and come back with the police.'

'Let's go.'

But it was too late.

Tides being what they are and daylight

being precious to yachtsmen, early morning departures are often the order of the day. In the breaking dawn the ketch *Angélique* of Brest lay quiet and enigmatic as the Mona Lisa, but the tide under her keel was urging her out to sea and causing her to tug at her moorings like a child impatient to get away from its apron strings.

When Martin opened the hatch to get away he heard the noise of a car engine and something moving caught his eye. He saw that a van had come into the yard and was coming down to the waterfront. He ducked down and, looking through one of the ports, he and Linda watched two indistinct figures unload some cases that looked like stores or provisions.

'We'd better hide,' he whispered.

'Sure.'

At first there seemed nowhere. No spacious holds, no room under bunks, behind machinery, on top of cupboards — in small yachts fittings are compact, close, maximising space, minimising movement in a seaway. Then they found somewhere. A narrow hanging wardrobe had been built into a corner of the forward cabin. Pushing two anoraks on hangers towards the door, they climbed in one after the other and, pressed together they just fitted. With the door shut they heard nothing very clearly, but confused sounds indicated that the people from the van were bringing their baggage aboard.

Then after a few moments of quiet there was the sound of voices, objects being shifted, movement on deck, the rustle of sails, one person calling to another, the noise of an engine firing, picking up and throbbing steadily. Then came the thump of ropes on deck, the heavier sound of an engine in gear and with it, a feeling of movement as the yacht evidently left the jetty and headed out into the stream.

In the dark of the wardrobe Linda squeezed Martin's hand and whispered into his ear. 'What do we do now?'

'I don't know,' Martin whispered back. 'Let's wait.'

The boat continued on its way. In a while there came the sound of sails being hoisted and after another interval the engine was shut off. In the quiet that followed the bustle and splash of the boat through the water came to them more strongly, but the motion was easier. Then finally after more time, they felt the bows heave and lift and dip as the yacht came out of the shelter of land and into the ocean swell.

Martin and Linda's confined quarters were becoming untenable. The air was getting closer and hotter and shortly they would be unable to move their cramped limbs. The longer they put off confronting the people who were sailing the yacht, the less they would be able to do so on equal terms.

'We'll have to move,' whispered Martin and pushed the door open gradually, gently. Carefully they stepped out into the forward cabin and stretched their limbs. Then when Linda pushed the cupboard door shut, out of the way, it uttered a high squeak.

'What's that? Who's there?' a man's voice called out from the cockpit.

Martin pulled open the door to the main cabin, and they stood in the growing morning light looking through the boat at the other occupants, a man and a woman. The woman was standing in front of the cooker heating some food; the man was outside in the cockpit looking through at them. He had a gun in his hand.

Linda and Martin had both been so sure that they were about to meet the Glazers, that the name was on Linda's lips. 'Greta . . . ' she began, but the word died almost as she said it.

For the two people were Bella and Ramón.

21

Out to Sea

Bella was the first to speak. 'For God's sake,' she said wildly. 'For God's sake what are *you* doing here?'

'We came to look for you,' said Linda. 'We thought you were dead.'

'I'm all right. Just leave me alone.'

'We've been worried sick. Why didn't you phone or write or anything?'

'Leave me alone. I'm OK. I'm enjoying . . . I wanted to get away . . . '

'Did the Glazers give you trouble? We wondered if they were into drugs . . . did they . . . '

'Just lay off her,' Ramón broke in with a hint of menace in his voice. 'This isn't a grilling.'

'Look — ' Bella spoke jerkily as if the words were forced out. 'You've surprised us . . . You must have forced your way in here.'

'You surprised us too.'

'You've jumped on us. I can't tell you . . . what's safe. I have to talk to Ray first.'

'What Bella says is best,' Ray was tense too. 'You two stay in the front cabin. We'll be back here. *Then* when we've talked we'll get together and settle everything. OK?'

Linda was going to say something but Martin stopped her. 'That's fine,' he said. 'Take your time. We're OK. I'm shutting the door and you call us when you're ready.'

They waited in the forward cabin sitting on the bunks for nearly ten minutes. All they could hear was the boat plunging forward close-hauled, presumably on automatic steering, and if they strained their ears, a murmur of voices.

'I stopped you,' said Martin in a low voice. 'I thought you were going to disagree.'

'So I was. The whole thing's crazy. Why can't she tell us? We might not be so close on some things since she's been away from home, but she is my sister after all.'

'I reckon Ramón was in a dangerous mood. He might have used that gun.'

'You're not serious?'

'Just something about him. I might be wrong. He's a funny guy. I don't trust him.'

When Bella called them and they all met in the cockpit, the atmosphere was more relaxed and friendly. Ramón was at the wheel adjusting the automatic pilot to a change of wind. The yacht had been lying close-hauled to a moderate sou'wester, now the wind had freed to the west and the yacht was travelling more easily with the wind nearly abeam. Bella produced bacon sandwiches and cups of coffee laced with rum.

'Sorry I was so edgy,' said Bella. 'But I got in deep with the Glazers. They got me into a drug racket. I couldn't write. They watched me, they were afraid I might give them away. I will write to Mom and I'll have to tell her that I'm staying over here whether she likes it or not.'

'It is her own life. She is grown up and a free adult,' said Ramón.

216

'You should have let us know before this,' said Linda.

'Where are the Glazers now?' asked Martin. 'They're not watching you now.'

'No, once they got me involved they gave me more rope. I've been handling drugs, contacting pushers. I'm not against it in a way. We're supplying a genuine demand and the government ought to make it a legitimate demand. They ought to legalise some drugs and make them the same as drink and cigarettes. You've probably guessed that I've tried drugs in a mild way myself. It's great. But I didn't want Poppa to know. Poppa wouldn't have left it at that.'

'But it's dangerous Bella — drugs!' said Linda anxiously.

'Oh, I can handle it. This voyage, I got Ray to come along. We're supposed to meet the Glazers down near the Gironde and pick up a load. But I'm going to break off with them. Ray'll help me.'

'You mean Ramón came over from the States especially?' asked Martin.

'I was coming over anyway — on business,' Ramón explained, adjusting the steering. 'We wanted to see each other again — very much. When Bella wrote to the address I gave her, she asked for assistance. One is always ready to help a friend. Now we are lovers and we will stay together. I can handle the Glazers for Bella. After this trip I will go back to my own work. There, now we are on course.'

They had passed the mouth of the Helford River and were bowling along south past Manacle Rocks. Soon after Black Head they would open up the Lizard, the last of England. The course Ramón was referring to was one that would clear Ushant.

'It's good to be sailing again,' Linda looked at the green shore, the white water against the dark rocks, at the sails and the blue sky. 'Seems I haven't sailed for weeks. I wish we could just sail and not have to bother about — the rest of it.'

'Now you are on board you had better come with us to France.' said Ray. 'We can drop you off at some port before we get to the Gironde.'

'That's an idea,' Bella agreed. 'We

needn't tell the Glazers, they might not like it. No one else need know.'

'Can we go with them?' Linda asked Martin. 'We left a bag at the boarding-house in Falmouth. We were going back this morning.'

'That's all right,' said Bella. 'Ray can get the hotel on the radio-telephone. He'll get through to the exchange before we're too far out and reception's still OK.'

'So — that should be OK,' said Martin looking at Linda. 'We haven't any other commitments. We booked out of the Club in London and I don't have to start work again yet. Let's enjoy some sailing while we've got the chance.'

'OK,' Linda agreed wondering what he had in mind. 'Do you know how we traced you?' Linda's head was full of doubts and unasked questions. 'It was through one of Paula's pieces, the Limoges enamel plaque. We managed to get the Falmouth address from Jean Fourneaux's office in Paris.'

'They shouldn't have given it to you.'

'Then you knew about it.' Linda

accused her. 'They didn't let us have the address. Martin got it by a trick without them knowing.'

'I knew *something* about it,' Bella admitted. 'The Glazers might have lifted some stuff. But it was too late for me to do anything about it. Anyhow Mom was insured so she wouldn't lose.'

'Why would they change the boat?' Martin asked. 'After all it did belong to them. And then hiding it.'

'I guess they wanted to drop out,' Bella waved an airy hand. 'They didn't want old friends recognising *Milady* when she was being used for smuggling dope, and they want to use the boat in France.'

* * *

So began what Linda thought was the strangest voyage she ever made. At the time they lived through it, the solid routine of sailing gave it reality, but in retrospect it seemed as remote and insubstantial as a dream.

22

Stormy Weather

They set watches, dividing up the night from eight in the evening until eight in the morning. The two girls took the first and last watches, Bella from 8 to 11 p.m. and Linda from 6 a.m. to breakfast at 8 a.m. Ramón took from 11 p.m. to 2 a.m. and Martin the remaining watch from 2 a.m. to 6 in the morning. They set no watches during the day. They would take the wheel and look out in turns or as the spirit moved them. They would share other chores such as keeping an eye on sails and on the automatic-pilot or checking the log or taking a reading of their position or direction finding.

Linda and Martin were to have the two berths in the forward cabin while Bella and Ramón had already established themselves in the after cabin. There was also the quarter berth in the main cabin near the cockpit that could be used for short naps during the day and at a pinch whoever was on watch at night might rest there briefly, provided they stayed awake and they were out of any shipping lanes and with nothing in sight.

While the girls prepared lunch, Ramón, evidently used to handling the radio-telephone, got the number of the boarding-house from the name and address which Martin gave him and finally got through to them. Mr and Mrs Firth, he told them, had unexpectedly gone on a cruise with friends. They did not want to keep their room but they would be back to pay their bill and pick up their luggage in due course.

The provisions that had been brought on board for the trip included a wealth of luxury items and they lunched on a pot of Beluga caviare followed by smoked chicken and a bottle of Château Yquem. They talked in general terms and about immediate practicalities, steering clear of awkward subjects. It was amicable enough but there was an underlying constraint on both sides.

'This is delicious,' said Linda helping herself to caviare. 'You do yourselves proud.'

'Ray likes to live like a prince,' Bella replied. 'He doesn't mind what it costs. Money's for spending is Ray's motto, isn't it Ray?'

'How was your voyage?' asked Martin. 'I mean across the Atlantic — weather-wise.'

'Pretty good,' Bella told him. 'Sailing so long and so far you feel you've really done something. Before that I'd just done the Virgins cruise and gone round the Chesapeake mud-holes. We had a storm about half-way, but it didn't last. Then another a few days before Plymouth but it was mostly with the wind behind us. We surfed along just under the jib for most of a whole day. The old tub was doing eight or nine — it was super. Not so good in the dark though.'

'Sounds great.'

'There was a bad eight hours when we tried to bash into it. That was in the first storm. A wave smashed one of the cabin windows and swamped everything.'

'Not so great.'

'You said it. Say, you two didn't come over here just to look for me?'

'Well, not altogether,' Martin told them about his insurance job and the ending of his Baltimore secondment. 'And it's our honeymoon too.'

'I'm Linda Firth, honey. We got married before we left.'

'Happy days,' Ramón raised his glass but made it sound half mocking.

'That's great. I saw the ring,' Bella said. 'But I kinda thought you might have put in on just . . . Me, I don't bother . . . ' she looked at Ramón.

'We *have* spent quite a bit of time bloodhounding around,' Linda admitted. 'We asked the police and the Customs and so on. We found the Customs man at Plymouth who checked you in.'

'We had a load of drugs on board then.' Bella tried to make light of it, but couldn't keep the slightly smug tone of the successful smuggler out of her voice. 'No bother at all. Then we went on to the Helford River to unload it. Then on to Falmouth where they did the repairs

224

and alterations. Then we went up to London.'

'There was one thing about the Customs in Plymouth that made us wonder,' Martin put in. 'Glazer's signature on the entry form seemed shaky. We thought of checking it with his firm, but the Customs man said . . . '

'You needn't take the trouble,' Ramón stared at him, expressionless. 'He'd hurt his hand.'

'That's right,' Bella confirmed hastily. 'I told Ramón. It was in the storm. He could use it but it was clumsy.'

'A thing I didn't know was that Greta had a touch of grey hair,' said Linda. 'The Customs man mentioned it. Also I saw two people in London I thought for a minute were you and Greta and that woman had some grey hair. I ran after them but I lost them in the Underground. Could it have been you?'

'She rinsed it and covered it up when they were visiting with us,' Bella explained. 'On the boat and over here she didn't bother. So it could have been us.'

'They were in London before they went to France,' Ramón amplified.

'So it's a small world — aaah,' Linda couldn't stop herself yawning. 'Gosh and gee, I'd be glad to turn in for a siesta. We didn't get any sleep last night.'

'You can all sleep. I will keep watch,' Ramón told them.

In the fore-cabin Linda and Martin lay on their bunks, exhausted as much by the unexpected turn of events as by the lack of sleep. Martin opened the two small portholes, closed the hatch and slipped the light bolt on the door.

'I wanted to come along,' he said, *sotto voce*, turning towards Linda, 'to see if we could find out more. I think there's something funny going on. Bella isn't natural and Ray hates my guts if not yours. I reckon they're covering something up. This business of the signature and the grey hair and hiding the boat. I wonder if the Glazers are still around? It's possible that Bella took those enamels. Well let's have a break from it now. Perhaps we'll find out in France.'

When they lay down *Angélique* was

sailing comfortably with the wind on the beam and steering a course that would take her outside Ushant if there was no change. By the time Martin came on deck again at half-past five the weather had noticeably freshened. Ramón was in the cockpit wrapped up against the autumn cold.

'Have you heard any weather forecasts?' Martin asked. 'There should be a shipping forecast soon — ten to six.'

The 17.50 forecast gave a warning of gales in the Sole, Plymouth and Biscay areas, the glass was falling and as time went on and darkness gathered, the westerly wind was backing further and further to the south. A gathering of black clouds brought stinging squalls of chilly rain. *Angélique* heeled over and became more uncomfortable as they brought in the sheets. They could feel her resenting it as she went head-and-shoulders into the rising waves. With a groan of timbers she would lift and crash down into the trough, then heel and gather way for the next effort. Things went crashing in the cabin, and Bella climbed down to make all secure. There were oilskins to go round and Linda and Martin borrowed woollen pullovers to put on underneath. The automatic pilot was having trouble, and they began steering by hand. By now it was dark.

'She's labouring like an overloaded horse,' Martin wiped off some spray and blinked his eyes. 'We ought to change down from this genoa before it gets worse.'

'Right. Let's do it. Bella, take the helm,' Ramón gave the order decisively.

Martin was as sure-footed as a chamois, and rarely needed to use a safety harness, but this time he wondered if he should. As they worked together on the narrow foredeck to lower the big reaching jib and hoist a small working jib, Ramón staggered about the deck like a drunken man, and twice barged into Martin and nearly knocked him overboard.

'She does bounce around,' he roared.

'*You*'re bouncing around,' Martin told him crossly. 'For God's sake keep a hand for the boat. You'll have us both over.'

'The chances are no good for a man

overboard now,' said Ramón savagely. 'Dark and stormy weather.'

'So watch it. Hang on.' A wave swept over them.

'I will change the lead for the new sail,' said Ramón, disappearing aft to do it, crawling along the narrow deck on the port side and crouching under the main boom.

Because the jib was smaller, the angle of the jib-sheet to the deck was different and, lacking a sliding track, it was necessary as part of the sail-change to take the sheet out of the old block further aft and lead it through another block further forward. When the smaller jib was properly set and drawing, Martin himself started to scramble back to the cockpit when Ramón, now at the wheel, shouted to him: 'Change the sheet on the other side please.'

Though not in immediate use it made sense to have the other jib sheet ready, so Martin bent down to do it. He had to work at a point where, with the cabin-top curving out, the deck was only a few inches wide. Suddenly, as he was concentrating on the job, the boat swung right round from the starboard to the port tack, nearly ninety degrees off course!

Since he was handling the loose sheet with both hands, the sudden movement threw Martin off balance. And when as a result of the 90-degree change of course, the heavy, metal boom swung over to his side of the yacht, it caught him full in the chest, and swept him over the side and into the water!

By good luck he was not seriously hurt or knocked unconscious as he might have been. He clutched at the yacht as it surged past him, but his fingers slipped along the smooth hull. Then his feet tangled in something. He was dragged along, his head under water, unable to breathe and he started to drown.

In the helpless position of being dragged along feet first he very likely *would* have been drowned, except that on the new tack the jib was backed, and the yacht, hove to momentarily, lost way and began edging crabwise, coming up to the wind and falling away.

Martin's foot had tangled in the line of

the log, which was trailing astern with a spinner attached at the end. It gave the distance covered and was a useful check on the electric log fixed under the boat, projecting through the hull. Now that the boat was for the moment no longer dragging him through the water, he was able to get his head up, get breath, reach down and disentangle the line from his ankle and hang on to it.

Having failed to drown him, the log-line had saved his life, since it had kept him with the yacht. Without it he would have been a hundred yards astern and, in the storm and the darkness, he would have had faint hope of being picked up.

Hove to, the yacht had lost way. Martin shouted desperately. The two girls appeared at the stern and threw him a heavier line. Linda found a bathing-ladder and was putting it over the side, but the yacht was plunging so in the heavy seas that the counter was under water at intervals, and Martin was able to wait his chance and more or less float on board. He shook himself, pale with anger.

'Who was at the helm?' he spluttered still waterlogged.

'Ramón . . . I . . . why?' Linda faltered.

He brushed past the girls and clambered to the centre cockpit where Ramón was standing at the wheel, and seized him at the throat through his oilskins.

'You bastard,' he shouted. 'You tried to drown me. You *meant* to drown me.'

Ramón with a face black as thunder tore Martin's hands away and threw him to the other side of the cockpit. The two men crouched, glaring at one another, both ready to fight.

'Stop, stop, stop!' The girls came scrambling from the stern, hanging on as the yacht lurched and rolled. As if by magnetic attraction Bella ran to Ramón, Linda to Martin.

'This is crazy,' Linda stood in front of Martin and faced the other two. 'We're in enough trouble already in this storm and just off the rocks of Ushant. We ought to be sailing the boat and making our position sure. We could all be drowned.'

'It *was* an accident, wasn't it?' Bella prompted Ramón.

'Sure, sure, an accident,' Ramón confirmed but in surly tones.

'It's his *machismo*,' Bella explained. 'He doesn't like to admit that he made a mistake.'

The two men could hardly fail to appreciate the urgent good sense of Linda's remarks. For himself Martin realised that whatever had happened, it needed the two of them working together to handle the yacht — and it was borne in on Ramón too. The wind was now howling in the rigging and the boat, even hove to, was still carrying far too much canvas. It was imperative that they should reduce sail. Gradually with both of them working, they got the mainsail reefed to a third and changed the working jib to a pocket-handkerchief storm-jib. Great waves rolled up out of the darkness and deluged them as they worked and the blown spray stung their faces. It was painful to look to windward and the visibility was down maybe to a hundred yards, though there were no

233

lights to measure it by. Martin kept as careful an eye on Ramón as on the ship and wore a safety-harness whenever he was out of the cockpit. But there was no further trouble.

23

Round Ushant

The girls got the boat sailing again on the same tack while Ramón and Martin, who had both been thoroughly soaked through, changed into dry clothes. Then after a general discussion Ramón took the helm and Martin took over the navigation.

'However, first things first,' thought Martin and poked his head up from the cabin to the others in the cockpit. 'How about a tot all round?' he suggested. 'Any rum?'

'Sure, there's a bottle of rum at the back of the galley stowage,' Bella told him. 'You'll have to use mugs.'

He found everything and passed round good measures of liquid sunshine which helped to lighten the gloom and restore them all a little. Then he made sure he had the right charts and turned to navigating.

Originally with the wind in the west and comfortably on the beam, their course had been set to take them outside Ushant. Ramón and Bella had not fancied going inside Ushant in the dark, either through the Fromveur Passage or the Chanal du Four. Also they had calculated that by the time they were near, the tide would be setting strongly north.

As the storm progressed the wind had backed round to the south so that now on the starboard tack they were not pointing better than 185° magnetic (less than 180° true). In the sea that was running, though the wind was pushing the boat through the water, she was making heavy weather of it and there was obviously a lot of leeway. Martin was sure they must be dangerously close to Ushant. It was urgent to get radio bearings to give them a reliable position.

First he checked the dead reckoning which put them some fifteen miles north-west of the island, but there was allowance to be made for tide and leeway and the time they had been hove to — all difficult factors to estimate. Another danger factor was that in such poor weather and visibility they could not rely on seeing the big light on Creach Point until they were right on top of it — even though it had a range of twenty-one miles. The same would apply to the lesser lights on Iles Vierges, Keréon, le Four and Pierres Vertes.

Almost completely discounting the dead reckoning then, Martin got out the portable radio-direction-finder. Working quickly with sharp ears and practised hands he got a signal from Round Island in the Scillies and then a strong signal from the CA of Ushant. Now to give him their position he wanted a third station and he managed to get the VG of les Iles Vierges.

'Virgin Islands,' he thought grimly. 'Bella met Ramón on a cruise to the Virgin Islands thousands of miles away from here — and all our worries really started there. And they aren't over yet.'

The result of his three readings was not encouraging. Ushant was only just a degree to port of the yacht's pitching bows and only about five miles away.

Danger indeed. In a short time they would be on the rocks. He put his head out.

'We're not more than five miles from Ushant and on our present course heading straight for it,' he announced.

'Then we have to go about,' said Linda.

They had been having their troubles in the cockpit. The stern navigation light had gone out and, leaving the girls to take the helm, Ramón had gone aft to repair it. Somehow water had got in and while Ramón was in the middle of trying to dry out a wet connection, a big cargo boat came up from almost dead astern. For long breath-holding seconds while both its port and starboard lights were visible, it seemed to be bearing straight down on them. And they had no stern light.

They waved a lighted Tilley lamp, shone torches on the sail and had a white flare ready just in case. Then its green light disappeared and the bearing of its red light slowly altered. It passed across their stern and disappeared to the west. A lot of other ships had passed them, but they had been in daylight and not near enough to worry about. From this near danger they gauged the visibility at a quarter of a mile and as the rain squalls were clearing, visibility generally was getting better.

'We weren't speculating so wildly — about *Milady's* being run down in the Channel,' Linda thought to herself, but she didn't say anything.

As a result of Martin's warning they tacked out to the west. Gradually tacking and checking their position, the bearing of the Ushant radio-beacon changed from ahead to abeam and then abaft the beam — and they had worked their way round the island. None of them got much sleep that night and the watches they had arranged went by the board, though they took it in turns to lie down. They all felt better when, after midnight, Linda by some magic produced out of the lurching turmoil of the cabin four mugs of hot soup.

In the small hours, although it was still blowing great guns, the visibility improved again dramatically and at last they saw Creach Point light flashing twice every ten seconds. Then came La Jument with its three red flashes every fifteen seconds. Then farther south they would see the light on the Chaussée de Seine, otherwise the Saints — a line of rocks and shallows stretching far out from the land and the grave of innumerable ships. Once past the Saints they had cleared all the dangers and could go back to the starboard tack with the wind a point or two free while the lights slowly drew past them. This meant not only faster progress, but an easier motion, and the knowledge that they had sea room and instead of butting into solid water would eventually be able to run before the waves.

Towards morning, partly because of the heaving motion and partly because he was getting sleepier, Martin dropped a pencil from the chart-table on to the quarter-berth in the main cabin. He fished around the edge of the mattress for some time unsuccessfully, and before he found the pencil his hand felt something hard and curiously shaped and he drew out a bottom denture. He was about to call out to the others, when the absurdity struck him of asking three people he knew all had very good teeth, whether they had lost a bottom denture. He curved his hand round the denture, put it safely in his pocket and began to think.

* * *

Dawn showed them a desolate seascape. They were surrounded by mile on mile of monotonous, grey ocean sewn with white crests, that rose up then were blown by the wind into streaks across the downward slopes of the watery hills. The waves were tigers spitting at their foe. Above it all, the bleak sky clamped down its sombre lid, shutting them into a wet, cold, howling prison. The wind in the night had reached Force 10 and now was little abated. The little yacht — its mainsail and jib reefed down to hardly more than dishcloths — moved alone in a surge of water that sometimes pulled at the rudder with giant force. The automatic pilot was still far from managing the steering. Heaving billows pursued *Angélique* like demons, towering ready to pounce. Mostly at the last minute she would run and lift her stern and the baffled monsters would roar beneath her, but occasionally she failed to escape and the hammer-blow of a great sea would crash on the stern, run forward to the cockpit and half drown the tiny craft. Streaming with water she would struggle out of the smother and toil forward, masts and stays straining and taut. The shriek of the wind in the rigging seemed even louder now that daylight made the storm gods visible.

'How about a weather report?' asked Martin. 'We've missed the one at six-thirty.'

'We can get a French one,' said Ramón. 'Bella will follow it exactly.'

Bella went down and put on the earphones while Ramón turned knobs on the big radio. Then she sat there waiting.

'It's still a gale warning,' she shortly

announced. 'Force 8 to 9, 10 locally. But its moderating.'

'Thank God it's moderating,' Martin held on to the wheel as a great wave tried to turn the yacht broadside on. 'We've had enough of this. Go and get your heads down. Perhaps someone could make some breakfast in an hour or so.'

As the morning wore on the weather gradually abated. By noon it was down to Force 5. They were now well into the Bay headed for the Ile de Ré and La Rochelle. With the wind abaft the beam they rode more easily, though a mile away a cargo-boat butting into it and taking great fountains of spray over the bow, showed what the sea could still do, if a boat was stubborn enough to go against it.

Ramón continued in a dark mood, but he did his share of handling the boat. He spoke civilly enough when necessary and Martin avoided provoking him. Together they changed to a bigger jib and took out reefs in the mainsail. About mid-morning Ramón and Bella had a long discussion in the aftercabin, and then Bella and

Ramón got on the radio-telephone and called up somewhere in France, since she spoke to someone at some length in rapid and voluble French. Neither Linda nor Martin caught more than the occasional word.

'That was our French connection,' she explained when Linda asked. 'We couldn't get through to Glazer. I said we'd been in a storm. The stern-light's OK now, but I made it an excuse to stop at La Rochelle, and said we'd push on to Royan as soon as possible. The Glazers know about Ray but they'd better not know about you.'

After lunch Linda and Martin retired to the forward cabin.

'Say,' Martin spoke in a low voice. 'They're both in the cockpit aren't they? Can't hear us?'

Linda nodded.

'Take a look at this. I found it under the mattress of the bunk in the main cabin.'

He brought out the denture so she could see it then stuffed it into his pocket again.

Linda exclaimed, 'It's somebody's false teeth! But it can't be anybody who's on board now,' she said looking puzzled.

'I reckon they might be Glazer's. He wore dentures all right and he sometimes slept on that bunk. But he wouldn't walk off the boat and leave them. Would he now?'

'Not unless he had another set. Or unless they belonged to someone else. Bella would know more.'

'Be very, very careful what you say to Bella. And don't say a word to Ray. For all they talk about them as accomplices, I reckon the Glazers might be dead. Dead men tell no tales and wear no dentures.'

'But Bella wouldn't be mixed up in anything like that! Dammit, she's my sister.'

'I don't mean doing anything directly herself. But she might know, might be involved — on drugs, infatuated with Ray, half willing.'

'Oh dear, I hope not.'

'There's another thing. While I was looking at the charts on board during the night I saw the one that was used crossing the Atlantic to England, and the noon positions are marked by tiny crosses all the way across.'

'Oh, are they? I seem to remember Glazer showing us . . .'

'Yes, so do I. Glazer showed his chart across from England to the States to us both once, and the midday positions were marked by dots.' When I looked more carefully at the chart on board I could see that there are dots underneath the crosses as far as Bermuda. It looks as though somebody else took over the navigation after Bermuda. But who? And why?'

'I'll have to talk to Bella. We are going to play along and get off at La Rochelle aren't we?'

'I think we've got to get off as they want. But for God's sake be careful what you say to Bella. Anything could be passed on to Ray.'

24

Boyhood

As a youngster the boy had had a tough for a father. In the slums of the town, his father Luis was known as a man to be handled with care. That is if you didn't want to end up one night with a cracked head, broken bones or worse. He was boss of a gang of workers, but with some undercover jobs on the side, and he reckoned to be among the toughest in a tough lot. Luis liked to boss people about and if it came to it, he had nothing against knocking them about too. With other men it didn't come to it very often, because either they kept on the right side of him or they could give him as good as they got. But with Luisa and the kid . . . well, it was just a question of keeping them in order.

Luis didn't beat the kid often. Only when he deserved it — like when he got fresh, or went round with the local gang, or when he hung around while Luis was keeping Luisa in order. Luis would start in on Luisa to stop her moaning about his drinking, or how little he gave her for food, and the little brat he'd hang around the place and try to interfere when he wasn't wanted. Cheeky he was. Didn't respect his father. Luis had caught him taking food, even money. Sometimes he worked him over pretty thoroughly. Really a pair like that, they needed it.

The kid hated his father and he wasn't sure he didn't hate his mother too. The way she took it when Luis beat her up. The way she gave Luis the best food and liked to see him eat. The way they got together in bed. Silly bitch, he'd as soon get away from the two of them. He grew up quickly. He was shrewd and clever. At school he did better than the other slum kids and he learned a lot from his father. He learned that if you got your boot in first you had a better chance of coming out the winner. That most people were scared of a real fight. That what people didn't see you doing they wouldn't blame you for. And that the easiest way out of trouble was to swear blind you didn't do it. By the time he was fourteen he was ready to leave home. He knew about girls. He had made it with Divina who was a year older than he was. He knew about guns too. Luis had a revolver he kept out of reach, and used it occasionally to frighten Luisa. He'd fire it into the air and Luisa would scream in terror and fall down and beg him to put it away.

The kid was bigger now, but Luis still beat him up when he felt like it. Then one day the kid had had enough. It was all in his mind what he would do. It was a night he knew his father would come home drunk. He helped himself to the money his mother had hidden away. The money she'd saved up, God knows how, and hidden away. Then he waited for his father with the gun and shot him as he staggered into bed. Then he shot his mother just to make it safe, and he lit out . . . He took Divina with him; he could make the big bitch do anything for him. No trouble getting clear away, the neighbours were used to Luis and his target-practice. He got lost in the slums of another town far enough away and the police never caught up with him.

Another town — a town with rich tourists. The stolen money was enough to set them up, to doll Divina up and make a real dish of her. He was a good manager and with encouragement she became a good whore. The money began to roll in. He took up drug dealing. He picked up another girl. He got to know other operators. He bought them out, frightened them off — all according. He ditched Divina. He changed his girls, his company, his habits. He cultivated an elegant exterior, hired teachers, coaches, got into sporting circles and in some sports became a keen competitor. He learned to mix in different levels of society in different countries.

But underneath the veneer, the charm, the expertise, he carried like lurking monsters the ruthlessness and violence inherited from his horrifying childhood. After all, what was killing a man? Simply getting rid of a rival or an enemy.

25

La Rochelle

By the next morning they were only some fifty miles from La Rochelle and had passed the buoys on the Plateau de Rochebonne. The weather, relenting, gave them a soft, sunny autumn day, all the lovelier for coming after the fury of the two previous days. The yacht dipped gently over a peaceful ocean, blown by a favourable breeze. There was a spinnaker in the wardrobe of sails and with enough wind to keep it full, it was pulling the boat along at a good five knots. Despite a nip in the air it was a pleasure to be on board.

The two women were on the foredeck on their own enjoying the sunshine. Martin had taken down the stern light fitting and in default of a new rubber gasket, he was treating the old one with sealant to keep it watertight. Ramón

was keeping watch in the cockpit.
Linda realised it was near the time
she would have to leave the boat.
Taking the opportunity while the two
men were occupied she turned to Bella
and addressed her '*Bella*' — in a certain
tone of voice that meant — let's have
a real woman-to-woman, let-down-our-
hair talk.

'Bella, can I make a telephone call to
Mom and Poppa saying I've seen you,
you're OK and you'll be back soon? You
did say you'd write but you've got to get
round to it and it's slower.'

'I'm not going back to the States,'
came the reply. 'Not for now anyhow.
And if I do I'm not going back to
Baltimore.'

'Why not?'

'Lots of reasons. I've grown out of it
and I don't want to live at home. I'm
like this (she pressed two fingers together)
with Ramón. I don't get on with Poppa.'
She hesitated. 'Linda we've never talked
about sex, have we, you and me . . . ?'

'N-ooo. Somehow it hasn't come up.
You've been away. I've never needed

to — It's great with Martin . . . '

'Well I've never told you about Poppa. It isn't easy.' She stopped again, nervously, twisting her hair round a finger. 'When I was fourteen — '

'You don't mean Poppa . . . ?'

'You know we all had separate bedrooms. Well he started coming into my room to see if I was up. Pretended at first that I was lazy and lying in. Well — it was an excuse . . . '

'Good Lord, you don't mean? I never had any trouble. He might give me a peck of a kiss, but that was it.'

'I think Mom was off sex, he was badly frustrated and it was me he fancied. He'd get into bed — to give me a quick cuddle. Ha, ha — if you please. And he — he started to masturbate me and get me to hold his dong. It never went any further because Paula came in one day and caught him — but it would have.'

'Good God, how awful. I'd no idea.'

'Why should you have? That's why I went to school abroad. There was an almighty row — hidden up of course. Paula had her ideas about culture and now she was determined to get me away. I can't say I minded. In a way it's put me against Poppa for good. Yet in another way it's all forgotten and I rub along with him. We didn't hit it off at times on the Virgins cruise, as you know. And look how they carried on with those tarts! Poppa was the ringleader. I don't think Paula goes for me all that much either. I'm sure there've been moments when she's been jealous.'

'Bella dear, I don't know what to say. I never even thought . . . Somehow I've never tied up the parents with sex. One takes it all for granted.'

'Well now I've told you. I suppose it isn't such a big tragedy and I've got over it.' Bella shrugged her shoulders dismissing it.

'But it's no reason to take drugs, Bella. They aren't the answer. You ought to give up this racket.'

'I don't want to, Linda. There's money in it — big money. Poppa's always kept me short. He can be a mean bastard sometimes. You don't seem to mind a modest job. Me, I want the big time.'

'Money isn't everything.'

'Then Ray and me we've got a principle at stake about drugs. Look how big business makes millions out of drink and cigarettes. Banning drugs, soft drugs anyway, is just arbitrary.'

'I hope you don't mean you're going on with — the Glazers and their gang?'

'I don't know. It depends on the terms. Ray'll be on my side. As I've said he doesn't disapprove of drugs. He's a marvellous lover and we'll stick together. Maybe this business with Poppa made me sexier, but boy — do I go for it.' Bella struck a Marilyn-Munro pose.

'One thing I still don't understand about this Glazer business,' said Linda curiously. 'I'd never in a month of Sundays have picked them as smugglers and dope dealers. They were such ordinary, respectable folk. He was a real fuddy-duddy — those false teeth of his. He took them out when he went to bed or lay down, didn't he?'

'Maybe he did. But what's that got to do with anything? Why bring that up — false teeth, dentures?'

'Oh, no reason,' Linda's unconcern was too marked. 'Anyhow if I can't tell the parents you're going back, I can phone and say you're well and I've seen you?'

'So long as you wait until you get back to London. Another day or two won't matter.'

'All right then. Oh look, that must be the Chassiron lighthouse. Gee it's good to see land again.'

'I'm going in for a gin. Gosh I wouldn't mind some hash. But that'll have to wait. Want anything?'

'Beer for me. I'll come and get it.'

The yacht was passing between the low sand-dunes of the Ile d'Oleron and the higher ground of the Ile de Ré. All four were on deck, gazing, looking through binoculars and enjoying the sight of land. Martin had found a Biscay Pilot on board which gave a detailed description of the passage through the Pertuis d'Antioch and the approach to La Rochelle.

'It's a good thing the storm didn't hit us here,' he said. 'In heavy weather the coast of the Ile de Ré is covered with spray and practically invisible. The sea breaks on the Plateau de Rochebonne and in bad weather from the west it is extremely dangerous.'

'What about the port?' asked Ramón.

'La Rochelle dries out at low tide. We're lucky. High tide is at 1600, it's now . . . 1330 and we've got about four miles to go. So there's time for you to drop us and get out again before low tide. I don't suppose you want to stay over between tides now the stern light's fixed.'

'Is that La Rochelle right ahead?' asked Linda. They were steering up the channel between buoys and Martin had the Biscay Pilot in the cockpit open in front of him. Ramón had taken over the steering ready to go in.

'There's a view of La Rochelle from the south-west.' Martin pointed out the landmarks shown in the drawing from the Pilot. 'There's St Bartélemy's Church on the hill to the left, La Lanterne and the church, then St Nicholas' Tower in the centre and the Railway Station over on the right — a complete picture of the town for sailors. The leading line to enter the port is 059 degrees.'

'Allowing variation I am steering 060 degrees,' said Ramón. 'It is spot on as you say. You should get ready to go ashore.'

'Have you got enough money?' Bella asked.

'We're all right, I've got a card that's good all over the Common Market,' Martin patted his pocket.

'How about passports?'

'I've got a Community UK one and Linda's got an American one. We had them on us when we left the boarding-house. Maybe we won't have to show them going ashore like this.'

★ ★ ★

La Rochelle is one of the largest fishing ports in France though the big commercial port is La Pallice on l'Ile de Ré. Ramón started the engine at the entrance, Martin and Bella dropped the sails and they motored slowly in. They were in by 1450 and made their way to the north-western side, where other yachts were moored alongside pontoons. There were no spare berths, but they went alongside another yacht with nobody on board and made fast.

'Here we are then. Journey's end for us.' Linda kissed Bella, Martin shook his hands with Ramón.

'Goodbye then, I hope you have a good passage to Royan.'

'Have a good trip to London. Maybe we'll see you there.'

'Don't make that phone call until you get to London, Linda. By then I could phone and let you know what I decide. Or we might see you.' Bella sounded vague and uncertain.

Martin cast off the mooring lines; Ramón put the engine in gear; the yacht moved forward and curved away from the pontoon. Linda and Martin waved. Bella waved back. They saw Ramón go forward and hoist the jib and mainsail while Bella at the helm kept the yacht head to wind. Then she bore away through the entrance and on a reach headed south — getting smaller and smaller until she was lost to view.

26

Shadowed

No one seemed to be at all interested in Linda and Martin, so having no luggage except a small haversack which Martin shouldered, they simply picked their way along the pontoons. They passed a building marked Club Maritime and found themselves in the town.

'Let's have a cup of coffee and talk,' said Linda.

They found a café, *Les Trois Anges*, with big windows overlooking the port and sat with coffee and brioches, warm against the autumn chill and content to be on land after their rough passage.

'First we'd better get our passports stamped.'

'Good thing we brought them.'

'Then we need some money — then what?'

'Martin, we can't just go back to

London and simply abandon Bella. We have to go on to Royan. She says she wants to break off with the Glazers, but supposing they don't let her — or persuade her otherwise? Anyhow, is it the Glazers? She's mixed up with some drug people all right — but who?'

'Hell, I don't know.' Martin admitted. 'I know I was pretty glad to get off that yacht in one piece — but I expect you're right. If we go on to Royan, we can get there well before the yacht and see what happens when they arrive. Keep in the background and do a bit of shadowing. All I know is — something possibly happened to the Glazers, Ramón is an out-and-out crook and Bella's hooked on him good and proper. There is something else we could do,' he added thoughtfully.

'What's that?'

'Go to the French police, report a stolen yacht, referring them back to Plymouth, and have Ramón arrested at Royan.'

'The trouble is Bella might get arrested too. I'm not turning my sister in — not unless I know a lot more.'

'That's it then,' Martin agreed. 'We go

on to Royan on our own and keep our eyes and ears open.'

They walked back to the Club Maritime and found a girl in charge who listened to their story as if it was the commonest thing in the world for strangers from England to come ashore at La Rochelle. She directed them to the *gendarmerie* where, after amicable exchanges, they got their passports stamped.

The banks were closed, but they found a bureau de change where they got £300 of French francs using Martin's bank card. Then at the imposing railway-station, they found that there was a late-afternoon train through Rochefort to Saintes where they would have to change to a branch line.

What they did not know was that a man waiting for the yacht had seen them come ashore and go to the café. He had followed them to the *gendarmerie* and then to the railway-station, where he had seen them buy their tickets. He had gone to a public telephone and spoken to a colleague. Then he too had caught the train to Royan.

On board *Angélique* Bella and Ramón had taken a course outside l'Ile d'Oléron and then on south to the Pointe de la Courbe. This outside route would avoid the hazards of hugging the coast on a falling tide with unknown currents and sandbanks and with darkness coming on. This route would only add another twelve miles in the distance, making it fifty-seven miles to Royan instead of forty-five. Even with light winds they ought to do it in fifteen hours at the most.

'So we have seen the last of them,' said Ramón with satisfaction.

'I hope they won't cause any trouble. They might be suspicious about the Glazers. Linda mentioned his false teeth in a curious way. He used to take out his bottom denture and tuck it at the side of the mattress. But how could she have known that? Martin did use the same bunk once or twice on this trip, that Glazer was sleeping in when — when he — he fell overboard. Suppose Glazer

263

wasn't wearing them — and Martin found it . . . ?'

'So long as it's only suspicion. I hope you didn't tell that busybody Linda too much and they won't go to the police?'

'No I don't . . . I didn't . . . She promised not to do anything, not even phone the States, until they get back to London.'

'Good. You know if anything about the Glazers could be proved, you'd be in big trouble. You could be charged as an accessory — to murder . . . ' punching the words at her as she stood at the tiller, Ramón put out his hand and though she flinched away, pinched her cheek and held her in a vicelike grip as he talked.

'No Ray, no!' Bella pulled away. 'I knew nothing about that — nothing. Stealing the yacht was one thing. I reckoned because it was insured, they wouldn't lose out. But I wasn't involved in anything else.'

'Well you don't want to spend the next twenty years in a cell. I don't know what you did or didn't do. I wasn't there. It was Karl and Eva. Now take one of these to calm you down — and give you a kick too,' he held out one of the pills he was carrying.

'I didn't do anything . . . I didn't, I didn't . . . ' Bella spoke feverishly and took the pill eagerly.

'What you need is another party with Karl and Eva. Just the four of us. You're their favourite girl, you know. Now we have to sail. You can go and lie down and I'll take over. But first let me get Karl on the telephone. I want to give him a message.'

* * *

The little autorail, just two walk-through carriages, ran through fertile French countryside with fields of corn, tobacco and rye alternating with market-gardens, vineyards, pasture land and woods. It passed through scattered villages where the local estaminets were fronted by arbours of vines, the stations gay with late flowers. They reached the town of Rochefort with its new blocks of flats, its church and château, then clattered across

265

the broad river. By six o'clock they were in Saintes with ten minutes to wait for a train to Royan. The second train was less crowded and seemed to go slower. They travelled on through a red sunset and lights began to appear at the stations and in the houses as evening gathered.

'Linda,' Martin leaned over so only she could hear, 'I don't want to scare you, but I reckon we're being followed. There's a man on this train I saw down near the docks at La Rochelle, then at the railway station there, then again when we changed trains at Saintes. That's quite a few coincidences. He looks a tough guy and I think he got into the next carriage.'

'Do you think Ray got a message through on the radio-telephone? He talked as well as Bella. What can we do about it? Give up and take a train to London from Royan?'

'Let's try and give him the slip at Royan. I want to know what *Angélique* does.'

'Except for Bella we could go back to London and forget the whole thing.'

'Do you think we could confront the chap who's following us?' Martin mused. 'No it wouldn't work. He looks strong and beefy, our French isn't good enough and it wouldn't stop him trying to follow anyhow. If we gave him the slip . . . go into a store say and slip out a back way . . .'

'All the shops will be shut,' pointed out Linda, always practical.

'A café then . . . I know. We decide where to stay first, then we separate. That'll fox him. Whoever he follows skips into a café and out a back way. The other one goes to the hotel we've decided on and we finally meet there. How about that?'

'We've done some mad things lately. Why should we stop now? Let's try it.'

'All right, it's on. There he is.' As they got out of the train at Royan, Martin indicated a big, strong young man with dark, short hair.

Doing anything but look in their direction the man joined the throng at the exit. They wandered into the glitter of bustling, modern, tourist-orientated

Royan, their shadow following them at a reasonable distance. They picked out a modest hotel, *Le Palais*, in a side street, but not far from the port and the fashionable *plage*. Then at a corner past the hotel they said *au revoir* and parted, Linda taking a right-hand turning and Martin going down the street straight on.

After a moment's hesitation the man followed Martin, who as soon as he realised it, began to look for a suitable café. He came to a large square, Place de Lafayette, which had several cafés but one larger than the others and well patronised, the Café de Bordeaux. Though, like most French cafés, you could see into it from the street, Martin reckoned that his half-minute's start on his pursuer would be enough and went in. He went straight towards the back and asked a waiter with drinks, '*Le lavabo s'il vous plaît.*'

The man looked at him, then registered, '*Ah, les toilettes. Par là —* ' he indicated with his free hand.

Martin dived down a dimly-lit passage, passed a door marked *Toilettes* and continued on. At the end a door led out into a yard lit by an outside light-bracket, with neatly stacked crates and a belated climbing rose in one corner. A young woman had just come in from the street and was parking a bicycle. Flinging a *'bonsoir mademoiselle'* at the surprised girl, he hurried out through the half-open gate into the street beyond. It was a *cul de sac* and it led into a street at the back of the Place de Lafayette. He gave a satisfied grunt and, asking directions, found his way back to the *Hôtel du Palais*. Linda was waiting for him in the foyer and together they booked a room for the night. Martin was cock-a-hoop.

'It worked! It worked like a dream. I'll be applying for Scotland Yard next. As easy as cutting your American layer cake. Now let's go out and see what we can get to eat in this seaside resort.'

Being out of season they got seated straight away at a good-looking restaurant and had the *menu gastronomique* at a hundred-and-seventy francs a throw with *vin compris* and *langouste à la mode de Royan* for the main course.

Their appetites might have been less hearty if they had known that the man who had followed them was checking the hotels in the town to see if his friends, the Firths, *un Anglais et une Americaine*, had booked a room. Before they got their *café filtre*, he had found their names at *Le Palais*.

'*Non, non, ce n'est pas la peine*,' he told the reception when they asked if he would leave a message. '*Je reviendrai demain.*'

27

Hit and Run

Linda and Martin woke about 7.30 in the morning and repeated their love-making of the night before, since they both felt a healthy edge of desire. Nothing had been possible on board the yacht for the past days in such weather and with the situation so tense between them and the other two. So they made up for lost time.

Then they had coffee and croissants in their room and lingered over the luxury of breakfast-in-bed. The yacht was not likely to get in before lunch, but Martin suggested a reconnaissance of the port in the morning.

'Better keep an eye out for the man who followed us,' Linda suggested. 'He's sure to be looking out for us.'

'I hope we've given him the slip. Might be a good thing to keep to the back streets though.'

It was when they were walking in a back street that the accident happened — a street deserted and with no pavements. The car came at them from behind, fast and with no warning.

Martin, hearing its engine, had a sudden premonition of danger. He acted quickly, yelled — 'Look Out!' — at the top of his voice, pushed Linda and flung himself aside.

But he was too late. The bonnet of the car caught them, flung them into the air and one of its back wheels hit Linda. Then leaving their two bodies lying on the road, it drove on at top speed and disappeared.

★ ★ ★

About the same time that morning, Ramón on board *Angélique* was again talking to Karl on the radio-telephone. The yacht had made a slowish passage with falling winds and an adverse tide and still had four hours to go before reaching Royan. Not wanting to be heard, he lowered his voice and turned up music on a radio to prevent Bella hearing his conversation.

'Hullo Ray, glad you called,' Karl sounded in good spirits. 'When will you make it to Royan? We've got the stuff ready to transfer on board. Ken is ready to sail her back.'

'We'll be there by two-thirty — say three. How about our friends who got off at La Rochelle?'

'Just as you expected — they didn't go back to London. We're taking care of them — good care.'

'You know it's really serious. They're half on to the Glazers. It's not just this yacht. If the police really got on to this one, they might start to investigate others over there. It might spoil all our plans on this side as well. It's important to look after them good and proper.'

'Don't worry. We're arranging an accident — a serious accident. I'll tell you more when you arrive.'

'OK.'

'When you do arrive, don't go into the port. We'll watch out and then come out to meet you. Then just follow us up river. We want a quiet spot for this job and there's a place we can anchor safely. Then come and moor alongside. Are you sure to arrive by three?'

'Sure. The wind might get lighter, but we can motor if we have to. And Bella needs a party. To relax and forget about her sister.'

'That's fine. We'll give her a big trip — keep her floating, keep her high. Plus a foursome on board here. Eva'll cheer her up.'

★ ★ ★

Martin came to, in an ambulance with a white-coated *infirmier* bending over him.

'*On vous croirait tous deux morts,*' he said when he saw Martin looking up at him. '*Mais nous voilà. Ça va. Reposez-vous.*'

Martin groaned. There was a dull pain in his head and his whole body ached.

'*Vous souffrez?*' the attendant sounded sympathetic. '*Nous arrivons.*'

'Linda . . . Linda?' Martin murmured weakly.

'*La femme?*'

'*Oui. Elle . . . est . . . comment?*'

A shadow crossed the ambulance-man's face. '*On ne sait pas. Ésperons.* We hope.'

The ambulance came to a halt. Two stretchers were carried out. Martin found himself in a casualty theatre with doctors and nurses going over him, talking among themselves, trying the movement of his arms and his legs. They undid a bandage that had been put round his head presumably by the ambulanceman, while he was unconscious. They shaved some of his hair then he felt some pricks as they put in stitches. Finally one of them spoke to him —

'Are you English?'

'Yes, English. My wife's American . . . how is she?'

'We will find out. How do you feel? Much pain?'

'A headache,' Martin touched his head. 'And my body. It is aching badly.'

'This will help the pain.' A needle pricked his arm and a warm tide of relief began to soothe away his troubles.

'How's my wife? My wife Linda?' he asked again more insistently.

The doctor looked at his colleagues. They spoke in French. One of them went to an adjoining theatre and returned.

'You were lucky, Monsieur. For you nothing serious — *rien de trop grave*. But for Madame — he made a *moue* and gave a slight shrug — her head is fractured and a leg broken and also injuries internal. There is some internal bleeding — we are giving blood by transfusion. What do you say in England — while there is life there is hope? She is young and strong.'

'I want to see her,' Martin started to get up.

'No, no, no, no. You cannot help. She is not conscious. As soon as she gets back conscious you will be able to see her. I engage. We are doing everything — *everything*. And you — I say OK, but you are deeply bruised and with a gash to your head. You must repose.'

Transferred to a hospital ward and allowed to get into bed, Martin lay full of a dull rage mixed with a gnawing anxiety about Linda. Those bastards. He knew now that Ray had knocked him overboard deliberately. They were killers. He was all right, but it looked as though they might have done for Linda. And her sister was in with them. What a business. No doubt they would keep Bella in the dark and keep her high on drugs and sex. And maybe threaten her a bit if she didn't cooperate.

If he was going to get back at them he had to find out what was going on. He *had* to be there when *Angélique* came in. Otherwise they might disappear altogether. Perhaps this was the opportunity now when they thought they had killed or at least immobilised them both.

Now if he could only trace their headquarters, he might get an opportunity to sink their boat, hand them over to the police, anything, anything for revenge. He wasn't going to give up and stay there, perhaps a sitting duck. There could be another attack out of the blue even while they were in hospital.

One thought filled his mind — to revenge Linda.

He hardly thought of the fact that he was unarmed, that he spoke little French, that he had been bruised, battered, knocked unconscious in an accident.

Now that the injection had taken its full effect he felt remarkably comfortable. He had been allowed to walk to the hospital ward, had managed to get along fairly well on his own two feet. His clothes had survived the accident and were stowed in a locker beside his bed with the contents of his pockets. He determined that somehow he had to get dressed and get away from the hospital. As it was he might be too late for the yacht. The ward clock showed one. If *Angélique* had got in during the morning and left again . . . but the afternoon was more likely.

Waiting until the nurses were busy with patients behind curtains, Martin slipped out of bed and with his clothes in a bundle, made his way towards the entrance. His bed was near the door to the ward and none of the other patients paid any attention. Once out of the ward he followed an arrow that showed the way to the main entrance. As he went he could see through windows that he was on an upper floor and that the hospital was near the port. He caught a glimpse of blue water and a motor-boat moving. He passed private rooms and what might have been a staff room with nurses inside, but they were too busy talking to see him.

Then came a bathroom and two WCs. He slipped into the second WC and bolted the door. In a few moments he had taken off the hospital bed-gown he was wearing and put on his own clothes — shirt, pullover and jeans. He still felt OK. In another minute he was limping as fast as he could down stairs and towards the exit. People looked at him, but nobody stopped him.

Then he was on the ground floor and mingling with the bigger throng of doctors, nurses, visitors and porters. He saw himself in a large mirror as he passed. He looked pale and had two

279

dressings, one over his right temple, the other at the side of his head. Really a bit of a disguise, he thought. Then he was out in the street and looking for the port.

28

Amateur Sleuth

Martin had to wait for half-an-hour watching from his vantage point, before his patience was rewarded.

The attractive modern town of Royan, largely rebuilt since the war, centres on the sea-front with its wide beach, bathing tents and promenades, and at one end the little harbour with a dozen fishing-boats and larger vessels tied up alongside the encircling sea wall. There are moorings for yachts in the centre and a pier where they can temporarily go alongside.

Overlooking the port is a modern complex built on a circular plan — casino, concert-hall, arcades, shops and restaurants. Martin found a café with a few outside tables and a good view of the port and beyond out to sea. There he sat with groups of late tourists. Hiding behind a local newspaper he slowly sipped a *demi* while he surveyed the port, its entrance and approaches. The injection was wearing off slightly and his leg was aching, but he felt all right to carry on.

The port was moderately busy, since it was approaching high tide. Two fishing-boats were getting ready to go out, another one was coming in and on the far side of the port away from the elegance of the casino and the beach, a fourth boat had begun to unload its catch. There were buyers and a transport lorry and market women ready to pick up smaller quantities.

In contrast to the fishing-boats there was a private yacht of about 100 tons lying alongside the quay. It seemed ready to leave as they were getting in the gang-plank and standing by the mooring ropes fore and aft.

Then he saw a yacht outside the harbour walls. The big diesel yacht let go its bow, moved out from the wall; then, its stern line gone, it motored towards the entrance. The yacht which had arrived and was now waiting outside the port, was *Angélique*, flying the French tricolor, her sails lowered and under her engine. The two boats passed near each other and there seemed some communication between them. Somebody on the big boat was speaking through a loud-hailer. Then the big yacht moved south-east along the north bank of the Gironde, followed in two or three cables by the sailing boat.

Martin watched with dismay. He thought Ray and Bella would come ashore at the port and he could follow them to a hide-out on shore. Now what? He stood staring as the two boats got smaller and smaller, heading up river.

They're not going across the estuary, he decided, to Verdon or Pauillac — so they must be going up the Dordogne side. But how far? To Blaye — or some quiet anchorage before that? It was now blowing a light north-easter so they could drop the hook anywhere offshore and be comfortable for the night. He tried to remember the chart of the Gironde that had been on board. There was a place called Meschers and another called Port Maubert.

Hell, suppose he went back to the hospital and gave the whole thing up. At least he'd be near Linda even if he couldn't help her.

But as he went over and paid his bill, he found himself asking the waitress for *les Autobus* (which it turned out were properly called *les Cars*) and once he had arrived at the bus station which was near by, scanning the time-tables. One route seemed definitely to go along the river since its stops included Meschers-sur-Gironde, Talmont-sur-Gironde, Mortagne-sur-Gironde, then several ports including Port Maubert.

Soon he was rattling over cobbled streets and then out of the town — but he found that for much of the route the river was hidden by buildings, and several times the road veered inland. He would have to get off periodically and search the river. At least even with the scheduled and sometimes unscheduled stops, he was travelling a lot faster than the boats. Calculating as well as he could where the boats might be, he decided to get off at Talmont-sur-Gironde, about seven miles from Royan, where he walked down to the river and waited.

After ten minutes there was nothing in sight. He didn't think they could have passed him so he decided they must have anchored further back, and he began to walk back along the road to Royan. Then he saw the two boats coming upstream some quarter of a mile from the shore. They passed him but going very slowly and Martin found he could keep them in sight despite his gammy leg. He left the scattered houses of Talmont and followed the road beyond for half-a-mile. It was low country and on the landward side of the road there were fields of corn, tobacco, orchards and some grazing land. Between the road and the river was rough grassland and scattered bushes and it was largely uncultivated. Ahead but some distance away he could see two windmills.

Then, just as he was thinking he would have to give up following on foot, the diesel yacht slowed still further. It swung into a small bay and came to anchor only a hundred yards from the shore. They were hardly likely to be on the look-out for anyone, but in case there was a colleague on shore, Martin dropped to the ground as he got near the river bank and watched from behind a bush. The yacht *Angélique* came slowly up to the bigger boat then went carefully alongside.

Martin waited for five minutes, but there was no activity, no boat being launched, no movement on deck. Whatever it is — handling drugs probably — it's all going to happen tonight, he concluded. It'll be dark in an hour or so and how am I going to get out there? If I could sneak on board in the dark, at least I could eavesdrop — I might get to the engines and sabotage them — or get to the sea-cocks, that would be something. But the way I feel now I can't swim it. I need a boat. Gosh, I wish I had a gun too. All I've got is a pocket knife and that's about at lethal as a packet of crisps.

He felt suddenly tired and despondent. His headache was coming back and one particular bruise on his thigh gave him no rest. For some minutes he lay, eyes closed, trying to relax completely. Then he crawled back, got up cautiously and got back on to the road. There had not been very many houses at Talmont, but there had been a café and a village shop which had seemed to stock a bit of everything. There looked to be nothing at all on the road ahead. So he slowly and painfully walked back to Talmont, trying to ignore the pain in his leg.

When he arrived in the village he first went down to the foreshore to see if there were any stray boats that he might borrow, hire or steal. But he had no luck. All the boats were too big and heavy for him to handle in his present state. In any case they were without oars and the lighter boats were also chained up. He decided he would try hiring as a last resort and he went up to the village store thinking he might enquire about boat owners. He also needed something for his headache and the pain in his leg.

It looked a well-stocked store. There were tins of food, fresh fruit and vegetables, stationery, newspapers, clothes, toilet goods, sweets, tobacco and toys. A middle-aged lady was serving and there was a woman customer who looked like a housewife. When she came to serve Martin the woman behind the counter looked at Martin's head and said in a sympathetic tone:

'*Ah Monsieur, j'espère que ce n'est rien de grave. Que voulezvous?*'

'*Non, rien de grave, merci, Madame . . . mais . . . avez-vous de l'aspirin?*'

'*Comment?*' Madame looked puzzled.

'*As-pir-in,*' Martin touched his head and then mimed swallowing a pill.

'*Aaah. De l'Aspirin — analgésique. Oui, oui. Vous êtes anglais?*'

'*Oui. Je suis en vacances. Un accident. Pas serieux . . . mais . . . douleur,*' he touched his head. Madame looked even more sympathetic and produced a bottle of pills.

Martin was about to ask if there was any chance he could hire a boat and was wondering how to put it in French, when looking round the shop his eye was caught by something in the rafters. It was a rubber dinghy already inflated, the sort that children can play with on a pond. It was less than five feet long, but it would do. He might even get out on a lilo, he thought, but this would be better — if he could afford it.

'*Combien?*' he asked, pointing.

'*Oh, très bon marché. C'est de l'année avant dernière. Maintenant ce sont beaucoup plus cher. Attendez —* ' she hooked it down with a pole. '*C'est trois-cent-quatre-vingt-dix-neuf.*'

'Oh — ' Martin looked blank.

'Ah, vous ne comprenez pas. Voici — ' she wrote it down on a slip of paper — 399 Fr.

'*Avec les —* oars' Martin made rowing movements.

'*Les avirons, oui. Et un petit soufflet aussi.*'

'*Je l'achète.*' Among what was left of the money they had divided between them in La Rochelle was a 500 Franc note.

'*Et ceci aussi —* ' He had found among the toys a child's cap-pistol — but it looked sufficiently like the real thing at a casual glance. '*Pour l'enfant,*' he added.

'*Très bien, entendu.*'

'*Et encore ceci — .*' It was a hank of cord.

Madame did some calculations. '*Ça fait trois . . . quatre . . . quatre-cent-quarante-cinq francs. Un billet de cinq cent. Voici cinquantecinq francs de monnaie.*'

'*Merci Madame. Est-il possible de manger ici?*'

'*Oui, au café à gauche. Au revoir, Monsieur. Bon chance.*'

Clutching his purchases and dragging the dinghy, Martin found the Café *Bon Accueil* just up the road near the church. Leaving the dinghy outside he ordered a sandwich, a glass of beer and a cup of coffee. After he had had several aspirins, he felt very much better.

It was getting dark now and outside the solitary street-lamp cast strange shadows in the little square. Inside the café there was a clink of glasses, voices rising to occasional argument or laughter, people coming or going. There were a few cars parked outside. Now he had rested he decided he had better get on with it.

No one took particular notice when he got up and left.

He walked down to the water. The tide had almost gone out and he could see the dark shape of the diesel yacht upstream from the village. Between Talmont and where the boats were anchored the falling tide had left uncovered a bank of black mud and sand that gleamed in an occasional light from the shore. If he tried to launch the dinghy there he might sink in the mud and he had no reserve energy to throw away on floundering about. He had better row along from Talmont where there was a rocky point and a tiny jetty. There was no tide to speak of against him and it would also be safer not to approach directly from the shore.

Outside the circle of the village square, it was a lonely, desolate spot. A boat might lie at anchor amid the shallows of the estuary, unobtrusive and unobserved. Except in the tourist season buses were not frequent and there was little other traffic. The houses were few outside the small village and any river traffic to

Bordeaux followed the channel on the other side up past Pauillac. The place was ideal for undercover movement: goods could be carried from a farmhouse; a lorry could stop on a road; a small boat could go ashore. In the absence of any suspicions or information received who would investigate? Even the presence of pleasure boats at the tourist centre of Royan provided cover.

He wondered if he should wait until later, but there seemed no point. So he carried the little dinghy down to the end of the jetty, topped up the air with the pump and launched it. There was no room for him to get his knees down in a rowing position, so he removed the tiny thwart and kneeling down facing the bow, used one of the oars as a paddle. The water was still and black as ink except for the reflection of lights from the shore and a faint light ahead from the anchored boats. There was no moon and most of the sky was clouded over.

As Martin got nearer to the yacht he paddled more slowly and cautiously. There seemed to be no watch on deck and as he came up from astern and soundlessly manoeuvred the dinghy under the counter of *Angéliquc* he was unobserved. Both *Angélique* and the big yacht had riding lights on their forestays, but otherwise *Angélique* was in darkness and evidently there was nobody on board. The other boat had some lights on deck, lights shining from ports and windows, and there came the occasional sound of raised voices and laughter against a background of music.

First Martin fixed the dinghy so that it might help his retreat if he got into trouble. First he tied one end of the cord he had bought to *Angélique*'s rudder, under the waterline so it was not visible. Then after paying out the cord he tied the other end to the bow of the dinghy. Careful to be quiet, he pulled himself up on to the afterdeck and the dinghy, as he had planned, floated away into the darkness, though it was still held by an invisible line. If he went overboard he ought, by casting about with average luck, to be able to find it.

Angélique, her fenders out and moored

bow and stern, nestled by the side of her big sister, like a foal beside its mother. Martin crouched in the cockpit for a minute to get his bearings. The other boat towered above him and he could not see on board or see through any of the portholes. He could see the name lit by a deck light — *Henrietta*. There was a short ladder hanging down her side, but he was afraid to use it in case it was noisy. He found if he stood on the cabin-top he could heave himself up on to *Henrietta*'s deck — but he would have to pick the right moment as he would be in full light and quite defenceless.

He waited and listened. Nobody. With an effort he pulled himself up by a stanchion and got through the guard rails. Moments later he had his face against the window of the afterdeck saloon and was looking inside.

The saloon was larger than he expected. There was a dining-table, easy chairs and a smaller table with a group playing cards, drinking and smoking. A radio was playing and there was a large television set in one corner. Two of the men were dressed in blue jerseys and jeans. Another man wearing a suit had his coat off. He had a holster strapped on with a gun that fitted snugly under his arm. With them was a blonde wearing a loose robe, round-faced and with big nervous eyes. Martin looked for the Glazers but saw no sign of them. Bella and Ramón were not there either.

He watched for a minute then stepped softly forward along the deck until he came to a door past the saloon. It led to a wheel-house and a chart-room with a companionway going below. Suddenly as he stood at the door there was a noise behind him — he turned and he was facing Greta Glazer.

No. The woman facing him in the half-light was someone else. She had fair hair like Greta, she was middle-aged and about the same build. But her hair had a streak of grey, her face was more sensual and she seemed slightly more athletic. Martin whipped out the pistol he had bought and held it tensely.

'Don't call out,' he told her fiercely. 'This isn't a toy. Who are you?'

The woman looked at him apparently unafraid. Her lips were even touched with the ghost of a smile as though she didn't quite take him seriously.

'I'm Eva,' she told him in a rich, honey voice. 'Who did you think I was?'

'I thought you were Greta Glazer.'

Her face darkened like the sky before a storm. Her eyes flashed dangerously.

'You . . . you're . . . '

29

Prisoner

Before he could even turn his head or get an arm up to protect his face, Martin was seized from behind by a grip like a steel band that came across his throat, while a fist like a hammer knocked up his pistol arm. Convulsively he pulled the trigger and the paper cap went off with a light — bang! The woman stepped forward and pulled it out of his hand.

'Gawd, it's a toy pistol,' she gave a half laugh. 'Hold him Jake. I'll go and tell Karl.'

The big man who had come up so quietly behind Martin held him as easily as if he were a paper doll. A second man came out of the cabin and all that remained for him to do was to tie Martin up. This he proceeded to do methodically by binding his wrists together with a roll of sticking-plaster as tough as any cord and equally secure.

Eva put her head up from the companionway that went down from the wheelhouse and said: 'Karl wants to see him. Bring him down.'

Martin was roughly half-pushed, half-kicked down the companionway and into a cabin. In the eyes of the two who held him he was already as good as dead and they were not ones to waste gentleness on someone they were going to kill. He was in no condition to resist. His head and body were aching again and he felt deadly tired. At the same time the thought of Linda in hospital and perhaps fighting for life, kept his hidden anger as red-hot as the centre of a banked-down fire.

The cabin was an office with a desk and behind it sat a man with a heavy, saturnine expression and a strong body. In looks he might have passed for a tougher version of Eric Glazer. The woman who had introduced herself as Eva stood at the side of the cabin. One of Martin's captors marched him in and stood him in front of the desk with his taped hands in front of him.

'All right,' said the man. 'You're Martin Firth, aren't you? I'm Karl. How did you get here?'

Martin looked at his questioner and said nothing. The man who had brought him in swung his arm and slammed Martin across the face with a force that made his already aching head explode with pain. He shut his eyes and rocked on his feet.

'All right,' said the man Karl. 'Leave him alone, Jake. He doesn't look to be in too good shape. Give him a chair. He must have come out by boat as he isn't wet. Look all round and see if you can find a dinghy.'

'I did come out by dinghy,' said Martin quickly. 'But I lost the painter when I was getting on board. It floated away.'

'Just look round all the same, Jake. Now . . . ' he turned to Martin. 'Let's have a friendly talk. Why did you come here?'

'I came to look for the Glazers. I thought I might go in with them in the dope business.'

'We've taken over from the Glazers.'

'You mean you've bloody murdered them,' Martin burst out incautiously, unable to help himself. 'Like you tried to murder Linda and me.'

'You might as well know, since you won't be passing it on,' Karl said levelly. 'We took over their yacht. It's one of our sidelines. You see, genuine yachts, crewed by genuine sailors who do genuine cruises, are ideal for drugs. The narcotic boys are hot on lorries and commercial vessels — and fast motorboats doing short hops. So we go in for slow yachts doing longer passages. It's worked pretty good on the American side and we've got a nice little bunch operating. It's a fleet we've inherited, you might say. Boats that we've adapted and renamed because their owners don't want them any more. Now we're starting up on this side. It pays to be multinational. You have to consider the tax angle and laundering the money.'

'You sound a right set of thugs,' said Martin, 'just right for smuggling and selling drugs.'

'If you want to go into the dope business why don't you join us? Your girl could come in too. Where is she, by the way?'

'She — you can go to hell.'

'Not saying, eh. You think we might not have her best interests at heart. Of course there aren't many hospitals in Royan. We can find out where she is and send her some flowers. Or auntie and uncle could call to see her and take some presents along. And as for you, Mister. I don't think you'd fit into our operation after all. Some people aren't adaptable. You'll have to swim for it — but not here, we're too close in. Tomorrow when we put out to sea.'

The big man called Jake came back and reported: 'There's no dinghy tied up, boss. I looked round the two boats with a torch.'

'OK, Jake. Take him up and lock him in the store-room near the stern. It'll be handy when he has to go overboard. In the meantime he can enjoy the party music next door.'

As Karl had gone on about Linda,

Martin's heart had grown colder and colder. Her life was in the balance now. Even if she pulled through, even if they didn't hurt her in hospital, they could be waiting to finish her off. She could no more collaborate with them than he could. They should both have gone back to London and abandoned Bella. That way they'd at least have had a chance of being left alone. Now his schoolboy bravado had landed them both in a death trap.

Black despair filled him completely and he hadn't even the heart to curse Karl as Jake dragged him away on to the upper deck. He was bundled into a little cubby-hole at the stern adjoining partly the galley with a strong smell of old cooking and partly the main saloon. It seemed to be used as a storehouse. Once locked in and in the dark, he eased himself down to the deck where he found room to stretch out his legs and something to lean his back against. He sat there in the thick darkness and tried not to think, tried to rest. The noise of the card-playing and of music on a radio came through the bulkhead, but he was hardly conscious of it.

His aspirin was in a front pocket and he could get his taped hands down to it. With his fingers he managed to twist the cap off the bottle and holding it to his mouth he swallowed several tablets. After a time, it might have been half-an-hour, he felt better. He tried to get more comfortable as he had been leaning against something cold and hard and curved — cold . . . and hard . . . and curved . . .

He twisted round and opening his hands as wide as he could with the tape, he felt what he had been leaning against — three tall, round metal cylinders. It was just as he had thought. As a yachtsman he knew what they were, especially stored next to the galley.

'That's it,' he said to himself. 'I can take them all with me. Send us all to Kingdom Come. Blow us to hell and gone. Then if Linda recovers she'll be OK. She'll get back to the States. She'll find somebody else.'

A feeling of satisfaction and release

spread over him like a blessing. It was as if a long-suffered mental strain had been suddenly eased by the solution of a problem, the lifting of a burden. It was plain sailing now. Downhill all the way with a soldier's wind. He knew now how those *kamikaze* pilots felt. Once you've made up your mind to it — it's easy. It's peace.

He got up in the dark and turned, embracing and feeling the first of the cylinders with his hands. He might be able to find a light switch, but it wasn't necessary. He fumbled his hands over the top of the cylinder. There were round metal taps on the first two cylinders to be twisted open. The tapes on his wrists actually helped him to hold them tight. Anticlockwise? Clockwise? There — success with the first cylinder — then the second. On the third cylinder there was a rubber tube which led to the galley, to be pulled off. There — that was it.

There came a faint hissing of escaping gas. With the noise from next door it was not very noticeable. It would be cooking gas and whether it was methane or propane — it didn't matter. Both were heavier than air, both violently explosive. There was enough in the three big cylinders to blow up half-a-dozen boats.

Now he had to make sure the gas would leak through into the saloon where there were matches being struck, cigarettes being smoked. They had taken his toy pistol, but not the knife which was in his side pocket. Could he get his hand into that pocket with his wrists taped? If he pulled his jeans round — he managed to touch the knife, get it between two fingers and — dropped it on the deck. Sweeping round in the dark he finally found it and managed to get it open using his teeth. Then, guided by the noise, he knelt down and set to work with the little knife to gnaw a hole in the wooden partition nearest the card-players. Soon there was a little patch of light shining through from the other side and he managed to put the knife back in his pocket. The gas would go on and on leaking through that hole. Elsewhere the store was well enough built and there was a sill to the door which would keep the gas in as efficiently as it kept the sea-water out. All done — now he had just to wait. An explosion did depend on luck, on the gas being ignited. But judging by the careless voices thick with drink, the scrape of matches, the general noise of a heavy party — judging by these there was every chance of a match not properly put out, a cigarette dropped. Someone in the galley might even light a match later to see why the cooker had no fuel.

Martin was leaning against the bulkhead with his head in his hands and listening to the gas-bottles singing like serpents their soft song of death — when he was unexpectedly interrupted.

He was thinking tenderly now about his love for Linda. Thinking all the way through from the beginning: from the time they had met out sailing, from the time they had first made love in her nurse's apartment, from the time he decided that what he wanted most was to marry her — right up to the present: their honeymoon in England, their strange cruise to France, and now . . .

There was a quiet toughness in Linda, a core of independence, of spiritual strength, that made her good to be with. Perhaps that was how she differed from Bella. Bella — more beautiful, the toast of the town, the belle of the ball. But frivolous, vain, with unthinking enthusiasms and antipathies. Outwardly Bella was successful and sure, but inwardly there was a hint of extremes, hysteria, self-destroying weakness.

Just as Linda would never have attracted Ramón so she would never have been dominated by him. Bella wasn't criminal herself but she would go along with criminality. She must know about the Glazers. She must have kept quiet about that and she probably took the enamels. She must willingly or unwillingly be in a web of deceit. Martin guessed she was hooked on drugs and drowned deep in her passion for Ray. A luxury life mixed with drink, with drugs, with sexual ecstasies, with God knows what.

He was in the midst of these thoughts

when he was interrupted — interrupted
by the rattle of a key in the lock and
the sound of a woman's voice that called
softly: 'Come on out.'

It was Bella.

30

Climax

He went out into the half light of the deck. He was blinking but he managed to push the door shut behind him. Bella in a yachting outfit and a scarf over her hair, looked beautiful but wild-eyed, as though she was on some drug.

'You fool. Why did you come here?' She attacked him violently.

'We didn't go back to London. Linda didn't want to leave you alone.'

'Well get away. I took these keys. I'm doing this for Linda. Get away. I'll argue with Ray. I might get them to leave *you* alone if you leave *them* alone,' she spoke softly but vehemently.

'They tried to kill us. Perhaps they have killed Linda. She's in hospital.'

'For God's sake, you've got to get away. Get away now.'

They were standing at the stern and

hidden from the rest of the yacht. Part of the railing near them had been let down perhaps in readiness to load stores from a small boat. They talked hurriedly in low tones.

'I can't swim like this,' Martin held up his taped hands. 'I've got a knife in my pocket.'

'I'll cut you free,' she started sawing away with the pocketknife.

'Come with me, Bella.'

'Hell no, I like it here. Ray's the best lover I ever had. He and Karl and Eva. It's exciting.'

'You've *got* to come. You've got to. The yacht's going to blow up any minute. Save your life.'

'You mean you've planted a bomb? You're going to blow us up? You're going to kill . . . Ray? My Ray?' she sounded hysterical.

'He might be a good lover, but he's still a thug and a killer.'

Bella looked at him with wild eyes and contemptuous scorn.

'Killer . . . then what are you? You fool, you can drown! You can drown!'

With uncontrolled violence she pushed him full in the chest with both hands. Martin staggered, fell back towards the space where the rail had been dismantled and with an inarticulate cry disappeared overboard.

Hardly hearing the splash, Bella, out of control, ran forward calling wildly: 'Ray! Ray! Karl! Help! Help! There's a bomb . . . Martin . . . '

Martin went under water a couple of times and came up with bursting lungs.

'If I don't keep calm I will drown,' he told himself. 'I mustn't struggle.'

Lying on his back and balancing carefully, he kicked his legs up and lifted his still-taped hands over his head so that he floated with his mouth out of the water. Cradled in this position he filled his lungs again and again, until he felt stronger and easier and had got over the sudden shock of the cold water. The incoming tide was carrying him steadily away from the two boats. There was little wind and the dinghy would have floated away in the same direction so he had a good chance of floating into it.

'If I miss the dinghy,' he decided, 'I just lie like this, but turn my head to the shore and keep on kicking and kicking. I should touch ground if I can last long enough. Thank God my feet aren't taped too.'

If he had had to swim on his own, he would probably have drowned. But fortune sometimes favours the foolhardy. After a long minute he felt the dinghy nudging his ribs and reaching round he groped about, until he found the painter.

Supporting himself with the painter between his hands, he looked back at the two boats. There was a light on the smaller boat and he decided they must be searching for a bomb which they thought he might have planted when he first came on board. Bella was so hyped up and incoherent they probably only half-believed her bomb story. With luck they wouldn't think of the gas cylinders.

He felt the water was loosening the tape round his wrists. He managed to get his hands either side of a rowlock on the dinghy and began to pull and roll his wrists until they were almost free.

Then it happened.

There was a great flash of light, the stern of the larger boat seemed to lift in the air and simultaneously there came the thunderous sound of a violent explosion . . .

Then another . . .

Then another . . .

There were other lesser sounds of debris flying, of wrenching and rending, of a surge of water, of a human scream . . .

The blast of the explosion came like a blow. Then broken fragments began to rain down and crash into the water.

Martin, head just out of the water, kept low and hid in the shelter of the dinghy, still hanging on to the painter which he now felt was free. If the explosion had been on land he would have been killed, but nearly thirty feet of water was an impenetrable barrier. A few yards away a sheet of metal plunged into the water. A smaller piece fell on the dinghy and it began to lose air slowly.

Hanging on to the painter, Martin

kicked for the shore guiding the collapsing dinghy through a sea of floating fragments. He touched one object and shuddered away from it when he felt that it was something human and fleshy. About halfway to the shore waves of water from the explosion reached him, the first one nearly a foot high.

Almost automatically he kept on kicking — on and on and on. Surges of pain and exhaustion passed over him, but he kept going. Then at last his feet touched. He could stand. His hands were free. He staggered through shallow water, finding it more difficult as he lost the support the deeper depths had given him. Somehow he got through a mud bank to collapse, at the end of his tether, on dry sand.

31

Lovers' Meeting

The hospital in Royan from which Martin had set out was the nearest to the scene of the accident and that's where he found himself when he came to, the next day. This time he found himself the centre of attention because he was the only survivor of a disaster that filled the local paper and dominated the news on local radio. Both boats had been sunk by the explosion and debris had been scattered half-a-mile from the river bank. Fortunately no other boats or people in the neighbourhood had been affected. Nobody knew yet how the accident had occurred, but an investigation was already in hand.

The police came to question Martin in hospital. Having no time and being in no condition to manufacture an elaborate cover-up, he stuck largely to the truth. He told them the whole story of his and Linda's visit to England to try and trace Bella, his sister-in-law. He referred them to the Inspector they had seen at Scotland Yard and to Pieter van Loon of van Loon and Bonnet for confirmation.

He kept quiet about the fact that he had been on board, merely saying that he had bought the dinghy — they could get confirmation from Madame who ran the little shop at Talmont — and was rowing out to the boats when the explosion occurred. His dinghy had been sunk by flying splinters, but he had managed to get back to shore. If the police had doubts about the timing they never expressed them. The matter of his discharging himself from hospital earlier was passed over. There was never any suggestion that he was responsible for the accident.

The precise number of victims was never known and some bodies had been simply blown apart. Karl's body and Ramón's were among those recovered. Months later Drew learned from his police acquaintance in Baltimore that mention of a Ramón Aragón had been traced in police files at Caracas. Karl alias Charlie Bergman, had obtained American citizenship ten years earlier. Five years ago he had been charged with fraud and manslaughter in California though the case had failed through lack of evidence. The boat repair premises in Wherry Lane were deserted and no staff or directors of the company that had taken it over were traced. Paula successfully claimed the plaque held by Jean Fourneaux but none of the other pieces was traced. On the other hand divers recovered over a hundredweight of drugs from the sunken yachts.

When Martin regained consciousness he felt as weak as a kitten, the adrenalin that had kept him going having ebbed away. His head felt better though he still had aching pains in his body. But for the most part it was not himself he worried about. It was the fate of Bella that lay on his mind.

If he had been killed in the explosion as he intended there would have been no problem. If he had been more violent and pushed Bella overboard instead of asking her to come with him she might still be alive. He tried to push the thought away but it came back to trouble him. He had to face the fact that she had saved his life — and she had been killed. What would he say to Paula and Drew — and to Linda? It would have to be accepted as part of the whole wretched business.

When a nurse came to see him, his first words were to enquire about Linda.

'*Elle fait du progrès. On est content*', the sister told him. Later he was able to have a longer talk with a doctor.

'She has come out of danger. The fracture head — she has become conscious. But we keep her resting and sleeping. The internal bleeding is stopped. Her leg is not good. We must operate, but at present she cannot suffer that. As soon as possible. I hope successful, but maybe she will have a small limp. We have a good surgeon.'

'When can I see her?'

'Ah you should. It will help. I will ask Sister Agnes to arrange this afternoon. And yourself, you are OK? You must rest some days, but you can walk a little.

Then a final check on your head.'

'And can I send a cable to America?'

'Yes, yes, ask the sister.'

Martin started writing a cable: Found Bella with Ray in France. Had car accident. Linda and Martin in hospital recovering Will be OK. But Bella — He looked at what he had written, scribbled it all out and asked the sister if he could make a phone call to Baltimore in the States.

'*Vous voulez téléphoner aux Etats Unis? Mais — qui va payer?*'

'*Je téléphonerai* collect — reverse the charges collect . . . '

'Collect? *Qu'est-ce-que c'est?*'

'*C'est sens dessus-dessous. La personne en Amérique payerai.*'

'*Ah, c'est p.c.v. — payable chez vous. Compris. En ce cas d'accord.*'

By this time, however, it was twelve noon and Martin realised it would be six o'clock in the morning in Baltimore. With such a difficult message to deliver, he could hardly begin by waking them up. He would do it after he had seen Linda. At least they would have had breakfast and also he could give them the latest news about Linda herself.

That afternoon a nurse took him to the intensive care unit where Linda was in a room by herself. She was perfectly conscious but still under some sedation. There was a tube with a drip to her right arm, her head was swathed in a bandage and there was a large cage over her legs.

When she saw him her face lit with a radiant smile and her eyes never left him. He took her free hand, leaned over and gently kissed her on the lips. At the same time he felt a prick of tears start to his eyes — tears of gladness and sympathy.

'Darling, darling . . . Linda it's good . . . ' his voice was husky, 'Good to see you.'

'You've got some bandages too.' She looked at his head and the smile left her lips though not her eyes.

'It's nothing. Up there it's all best solid ivory so things just bounce off. You're the one we have to take care of.'

'What happened, Martin? Will they try again?' No smile now.

'I followed them, honey. I got out to their big boat.'

'You did? Who — were the Glazers there?'

'No. The Glazers are dead. I saw another chap, a creep called Karl. There was an explosion. I got away but the gang were all killed.'

'Bella?'

'It's bad news. I'll tell you.' Slowly he told her the whole story right to the end, to his last conversation with Bella and his swim to the shore. She listened absorbed, taking it quietly, outwardly calm — though occasional pressure from the hand he was holding showed her feelings.

'After they ran you down, honey, I was crazy, angry. I wasn't rational — just mad — mad in both senses I think now. It's Bella I'm sorry about. I might have saved her.'

Linda was silent for a while.

'I'll never blame you for what you did,' she said at last. 'They'd have been after us. I believe in friendship and kindness. But there's a time you've got to fight if the other folk are real mean.'

'I was lucky.'

'You did what you could about Bella. You can only ask people, not force them. Maybe I shouldn't say this — but I don't know that Bella had as much to look forward to as she thought. Not in the long run. Not like me.'

'Me too.' Their hands clasped more firmly and they were silent for a moment.

'I'm calling Paula and Drew later on,' said Martin at last. 'I feel I ought to phone them.'

'Gosh, you've got that chore too. Glad it's not me has to tell them. Good luck with it. Give my love.'

'Of course I will.'

'I guess we'll have them flying over and Poppa trying to organise everything. Maybe he tried to organise us girls too much. And *he* went crazy, another sort of crazy — what he did to Bella. I'll tell you about it some time. Well . . . ' she seemed to brood for a while.

'Darling, you rest,' Martin felt she had had enough.

'I can, now that I know you're around.'

'I'll be around — a long time.'